CRAZY EIGHTS
JAMES MELZER

SEVERED PRESS
HOBART TASMANIA

CRAZY EIGHTS

Copyright © 2017 James Melzer
Copyright © 2017 by Severed Press

WWW.SEVEREDPRESS.COM

All rights reserved. No part of this book may be reproduced or transmitted in any form or by any electronic or mechanical means, including photocopying, recording or by any information and retrieval system, without the written permission of the publisher and author, except where permitted by law. This novel is a work of fiction. Names, characters, places and incidents are the product of the author's imagination, or are used fictitiously. Any resemblance to actual events, locales or persons, living or dead, is purely coincidental.

ISBN: 978-1-925597-43-1

All rights reserved.

PROLOGUE

One thing Buckeye loved was taking a shit in the woods.

He tugged on the leash, his four paws scurrying over the summer leaves and dried twigs as he yanked his owner along the beaten path that led further up the Allegheny Mountains. His golden fur brushed against the bellworts, capturing pollen that caused a slight itch to begin spreading. Buckeye paused, using his hind leg to scratch it away as best he could.

"Who's a good boy?" the man on the other end of the leash asked.

Buckeye panted. *He* was a good boy. For nine years he'd been a good boy, and he loved his owner more than anything in this world. A world that was small and large all at once. Small because sometimes it was only four walls with limited space to move around in, and large on days like today when those walls disappeared and he could stretch his legs in the warm country air.

"What a beautiful day, right, Buckeye?"

The retriever sneezed, turning his attention back toward the ground. He picked up on something—something familiar and exciting. The scent of a small, furry animal with a twitchy nose that always seemed to elude him. He tugged harder on the leash, eager to search out the rabbit so he could chase it, because he loved to chase things, even if they always got away.

"Whoa, slow down there, buddy. What's your hurry?"

He ignored the voice of his owner, scampering forward, his nose picking up the trail. It wasn't strong yet, but he knew the further along he went the more noticeable it would become, and from there he might be able to track it down and at least get a good look at the small animal. Even if he'd never be able to catch it.

"Who's a good dog? Who's a good dog? Good boy, Buckeye, good boy."

His heart leapt at the sound of his owner's voice. He loved it when he spoke like that. His normal voice was deep and serious, but when he spoke to Buckeye it changed. Became higher and friendlier. It made Buckeye feel loved, and he loved love.

He also loved rabbits, and the scent he'd smelled became stronger, just like he knew it would. He raised his eyes and looked ahead, hoping to get a good look at it. He scanned the forest, searching through the trees and brush for the little critter, but no, there was nothing. He dipped his nose, continuing to seek it out, and then all of a sudden the trail went as cold as that white stuff he liked to jump around in sometimes. Snow, his owner called it. He loved snow, and love, and rabbits, and shitting in the woods.

But this new scent, the one that replaced the rabbit, wasn't very pleasant at all. It smelled…dangerous.

Buckeye barked. No sir, he didn't like it one bit.

"Hang on boy, I want to get a look at this."

He looked back at his owner, who was holding something in his hand that he panned across the countryside, when really he should have been paying closer attention to what was in the woods. Didn't he smell it?

"God, what an amazing day outside, huh?"

It was an amazing day. At least it was up until a few moments ago. Now Buckeye wasn't so sure. This new scent was strong in his nostrils. It was old, and dangerous, and smelled like trouble.

He had to do something. He had to warn his owner because if he didn't he'd feel bad if something happened to him.

Buckeye barked. Louder this time. There was definitely something out in these woods, and it wasn't a rabbit.

"Quiet, Buckeye."

Quiet? This was no time to be quiet. How can anyone be quiet at a time like this? There was something…there…right through those trees. He saw it, coming closer.

Closer.

His barking intensified and he tugged on the leash. Whatever it was wasn't going to get the man who took care of him. Who fed him, and cuddled him, and threw the ball for him. That was his master, and he had to protect the master.

"What is it, huh? What's out there?"

Buckeye didn't know what it was, just that it was there. Right there. Creeping and sneaking, bigger than the two of them and all he wanted to do was protect his master and oh God, there it is.

It crashed through the trees, coming into view. Buckeye continued barking at it, and the thing hissed.

"Holy fuck!"

He felt the leash go slack and looked briefly to see his owner running away, then he turned his attention back toward this new creature. A creature he'd never seen before. Or had he? It looked somewhat familiar to him. Just bigger. It had a bulbous body, with four legs extending from either side of it. Legs that were huge and hairy and made dull thuds in his ears the closer they came.

"Jesus Christ, what the fuck was that?" he heard his owner cry out from somewhere far behind him.

It's a spider. That's what it is. He'd chased them down before at his master's request. Sniffing and squishing them from time to time so they wouldn't hurt the man he loved.

Get the spider, Buckeye. Get it. Good boy.

Get the spider. Yes, that's what he had to do. He had to get the spider.

Buckeye growled and snarled and barked, the golden hair on his soft body raised and ready. He drew back, and as the spider came closer he jumped forward as hard as he could, ready to sink his teeth into it. He didn't care that it was bigger than him. All he cared about was protecting his master.

He soared through the air, feeling the soft breeze course along his fur while his eyes fixed themselves firmly on the large spider. The spider that had eight eyes, all of them looking straight at Buckeye.

Then he felt something sharp pierce his torso, and he dropped to the ground. He'd thought for sure that he would be able to bite the spider, maybe even squish it, but no.

The spider had bitten him.

Now he couldn't move. Something hot coursed through his body. It stung, and Buckeye felt his muscles contract and stiffen.

He tried to shake it off. Tried to get back up and run away. It was only in his head, though. His legs wouldn't respond. They just sat there, firm and unmoving, and a shadow passed over him as he stared through the trees, seeing his master off in the distance watching him.

Then something wet and sticky began to surround him. He looked down, seeing his hindquarters being wrapped up in it. Buckeye had no idea what it was, just that it came from the tail end of the spider, and that it wasn't good. He looked out over the wide berth separating him and his owner, David. Images of kisses and balls and snow and rabbits passed through his mind, and he whimpered, knowing that he'd never get to see or feel any of those things again.

This was the end of his life, and as the wet, sticky substance moved higher and higher, wrapping his body, then his neck, Buckeye at least knew that his master was safe.

And for that he was a good boy.

CHAPTER 1

Emily Nite hadn't gone to college, so it never ceased to amaze her when she was invited to speak at one.

The library of Washington State Community College in Marietta, Ohio, was packed with liberal arts students and their friends, and for the last hour they'd been listening to her lecture on the cryptid history of the United States. For her it was a chance to enlighten the minds of young students and open their eyes to a world many of them didn't know existed.

For the kids it was a chance to kill time on a Friday night.

"So as you can see, dragons aren't just native to Asian and European folklore." She paced back and forth in front of the gathered crowd, trying her best to hold their waning attention. "In fact, in 1890 two cowboys in Tombstone, Arizona, claimed to have chased down a giant flying lizard that measured 92 feet. They shot and killed the beast, bringing a piece of its wing back into town. The battle was chronicled in the April 26th edition of *The Tombstone Epitaph*."

She gave a half-cocked grin to the group, seeing in their eyes the same look she'd seen in thousands of eyes before them.

This chick's crazy.

A few of them snickered, with a voice coming from somewhere in the middle of the group yowling, "Must've been some damn good moonshine."

Laughter peppered the audience.

There was a time when she was first starting out that Emily's posture would have stiffened, and the confidence she'd been trying so hard to muster would have fizzled like bubbles in a glass of soda, but that was then, and this was now.

Now she chuckled along with them, nodding politely because despite the attitudes of a few, she knew that at least someone was getting something out of this lecture, and that's what she always looked for when she was presenting. That one person she could zero in on and have a heart-to-heart with.

The one person that made her feel like she wasn't wasting her breath.

This time it was a man, sitting toward the back. He wasn't a student; she'd guessed that from his thinning gray hair and stout build. Maybe a professor? It didn't matter. He was attentive, alert, and seemed to hang on every word that came out of her mouth, and that was enough fuel to keep Emily going.

He raised his brow toward the heckler as if asking her, *What are you going to do about it?*

Emily rolled her eyes and shrugged. Why could she do? She could go on the defensive, maybe shoot back a sarcastic comment of her own, but from experience she knew all that did was instigate a snippier dialogue than she was trying to achieve.

Thankfully her time was almost up, so she turned, ignoring the moonshine commentator, and began gathering her things. A briefcase, three books she'd written on cryptids in American history including her most recent, and a plastic statue of a large dragon she'd brought along for show. It didn't really add anything to the lecture; she just figured that since she was speaking about dragons, she'd bring a dragon.

"Miss Nite?" someone in the front asked.

Emily turned, tucking a stray strand of red hair that had broken loose from her ponytail back behind her ear. She smiled politely at the young woman who'd caught her attention, and the girl in turn looked sheepishly at the floor while shifting uncomfortably in her chair. Emily took a step forward, acknowledging her further while recognizing a bit of herself at that age. Shy, compliant, never one to rock the boat. Despite the crowd of skeptics, she could tell this girl wanted to believe, but at the same time she didn't want to be singled out.

"Yes?" Emily urged.

The girl's soft brown eyes raised to meet her own, and she asked rather timidly, "Do you really think all this stuff exists?"

Emily's gaze flickered briefly to the man at the back, who'd leaned forward in his chair to hear their exchange.

Who is he?

"I think," she beamed, "that not everything in this world has been discovered. That there could exist creatures beyond our understanding that stretch the limits of what we perceive as reality."

She noticed that it wasn't only the girl and the man in the back listening now. Her words had grabbed the crowd, giving her the jolt of electricity she needed to finish with a bang.

"Biodiversity scientists estimate that we've discovered less than ten percent of the species on earth. Ten percent! In 2015 we discovered everything from ghost sharks in New Zealand, to Dracula ants living deep below the surface of Madagascar. Who's to say there isn't a bipedal primate that's escaped the evolutionary chain roaming the wilderness, or a great megalodon deep in the Mariana Trench? I'll go one step further and say there could very well be dragons still populating our earth somewhere, hiding, living in a remote part of the world untouched by the footprints of explorers. Remember, every great legend stems from some form of truth, and the truth is…we just don't know. But me?"

She looked from the girl to the man and out over the crowd of people. Their skeptical expressions shifted, perhaps coming to the realization that maybe—just maybe—this woman knew what she was talking about.

Emily grinned, looking back at the girl in the front row.

"But me?" she repeated, a little quieter this time. "I want to believe."

She winked, causing an array of kindhearted giggles to rise up as many recognized her familiar words. Laughter was quickly followed by applause, bringing the evening to a close, and students came to the front to thank Emily personally, and get their books signed. They were few in number, but they were at least a number, including the girl from the front row, bringing hope to Emily that the night wasn't a total loss.

In her line of work it was always hard to tell what she was walking into with one of these lectures. Sometimes she found a crowd to be completely receptive to what she had to say, and other times they shut her down within the first few minutes, being nothing but argumentative for the duration of her time. Once, in Philadelphia, a man called her the anti-Christ before spitting in her face, saying God would never allow such abominations to walk the earth.

She often wondered why those sorts of people even bothered to attend her talks if they didn't want to listen to what she was saying.

Such was the life of a cryptozoologist.

"Thank you so much, Miss Nite," the girl from the front row said, handing her a copy of *American Dragon*. "That was a lot of fun."

"Please, call me Emily, and don't ever stop asking questions, okay? Curiosity might have killed the cat, but it never stopped anyone from living an interesting life."

She signed the book to Sophia Núñez, handing it back to the shy, freckled student, who nodded politely and scurried away.

Continuing to answer questions for the better part of an hour, Emily noticed the man sitting toward the back of the library hadn't moved. His gaze was still fixed on her as she talked animatedly with students about everything from Loch Ness, to one boy's experience with a poltergeist—something that also resided in Emily's wheelhouse because although her official title was cryptozoologist, her interests covered a wide variety of topics, including the paranormal.

By the time everyone had cleared out, the clock on the wall was pushing 8:30, with roughly 30 minutes of daylight left to burn on the warm July night. Emily placed her dragon statue in a tote bag, grabbed her briefcase, and turned to leave, only to find herself blocked by the man from the back, who was now very much in front of her.

"Miss Nite?" he asked, though it was rhetorical. They both knew who she was.

Emily fixed her eyes on his weathered face, and though it had seen a good sixty years at least, there was no trace of an elderly haunch to his posture. No sign of weariness to him at all, really. She'd been wrong about him. He wasn't stout. Quite the opposite. He was heavy, sure, but from the looks of this man his heaviness could be attributed to muscle rather than the comfortable, soft mass someone of his age might've accumulated over the years. Dressed in a dark suit, he reminded her of a decorated general. Someone stately and defined.

"Yes?" she answered.

He smiled. Not with his mouth, but with his eyes. They squinted ever so slightly into warm almonds that glowed back at her, sparking a hint of recognition, and prompting her to think that this man could be anyone's grandfather.

"Do I know you?" she followed up.

This time the smile showed on his face. Thin lips curled up into a mischievous grin as he stuck out his hand. Emily took it, her fingers dwarfed by his.

"No," he said. "But I know you. I'm an old friend of your father."

She flinched. Her father? The two hadn't spoken since she left home at 17. It had been a while since she'd stopped to dwell on their severed relationship, but now those memories crept into her psyché, flooding her with feelings of anger, remorse, and fear.

"Yeah, well, if you knew my father then you know why I left." There was a bite to her tone she didn't mean to display, and she instantly regretted it. Still, after all these years, he could do that to her.

The man held up his hands in mock surrender. "Easy. I'm not here to talk about your father, Emily."

"Who are you?"

"Frank Tempo," he said. "I enjoyed your latest book, *American Dragon*. Quite the fascinating read. I've always had a thing for dragons, you know. Such remarkable creatures. Did you know that in the Celtic tradition if your power animal is a fire dragon it will help you overcome any obstacle?"

"It also serves as a protector," she added, much to the delight of the elder man. "Bestowing the qualities of leadership and mastery, as well as—"

"I see a lot of that in you," he interrupted. "The way you take control of a crowd when you're speaking. Oh, maybe not tonight, but that wasn't your fault. Some people just aren't ready to hear the truth, but I was at your lecture two summers ago in Colorado, and I saw it, Emily. You had those people on the edge of their seat like only a good leader can. Yes, I'd say you definitely have some fire dragon in you."

She felt the redness of an instinctual blush creep into her cheeks. Compliments weren't her strong suit, so when she received one it always made her feel out of place, like she hadn't worked hard enough to deserve it.

Frank Tempo waved away his words as if they still hung in the air between them. "Listen to me, huh? The ramblings of an old man."

Emily offered him a pleasant nod, appreciating the compliment even if she didn't know what to do with it. She shifted her weight awkwardly from foot to foot. "No, it's okay. Thank you."

"Is there somewhere we can talk?" he asked.

She looked around the barren library, at the stacks of books and the few staff who were prepping to close up for the night. "Aren't we already talking?"

A brisk laugh escaped him. "Indeed we are, but I'm afraid what I have to discuss requires a little more privacy."

Although he didn't strike her as someone whose mind might be going, Emily had been approached by men like Frank before who'd wanted to talk, and at first she'd obliged them, but after listening to crazy conspiracy jargon about fake moon landings and presidents able to control the weather one too many times, she promised herself she'd reserve her time for those who had a more controlled approach to the world.

The verdict was still out on this man.

"Mr. Tempo," she sighed, "it's been a long day, and as much as I'd love to sit and talk with you about dragons, I really do have to be—"

"You misunderstand me, Emily. I don't want to talk about dragons."

She cocked her head to the side, a bit confused but admittedly still somewhat intrigued by his presence. He knew her father, knew about her work, obviously knew his folklore, but if he didn't want to talk about dragons, then…?

"I'm sorry," she said. "What is it you want to talk about?"

Please don't say aliens. Please don't say aliens. Please don't say—

"Spiders," he said. "I need to know everything there is to know about spiders."

CHAPTER 2

Thirty minutes later Emily was sitting with a glazed cake donut and a large iced coffee, watching as Frank Tempo brought his own order to the table.

She'd followed him in her car south on I-77 into West Virginia, booking a room at the Comfort Inn along the way. Her itinerary included a couple days rest before flying out to Austin, Texas, for the annual Chupacabracon, where she was one of the keynote speakers.

Her mind had turned over the possibilities of his request while the GPS guided her movements.

Spiders.

It was an odd thing to want to talk about, and she couldn't even fathom what about them he wanted to discuss, but he'd captured her interest enough to warrant at least a coffee, and when he'd mentioned the Dunkin' Donuts that was relatively close by she couldn't say no. Their iced coffee was her downfall, at any time of the year.

Frank rested a leather attaché at his feet before relaxing himself into the seat across from her. They'd grabbed a corner booth in the otherwise empty shop, and he cupped his hands around a large styrofoam cup of coffee.

Emily took a bite of her donut, washing it down with the sweet taste of caramel mocha. "So, spiders," she began.

"Spiders," he echoed. "What do you know about them?"

She shrugged. "Not much. Eight legs, a web, itsy bitsy spider went up the water spout, stuff like that."

"How about in terms of your area of expertise?"

"What do you mean?"

"You know, folklore, myths, legends, cryptozoology. Native, of course—I'm not looking for anything Celtic or Greek or what have you."

She thought about it for a moment, recalling all the things she'd read over the years. Her knowledge was thin, but there were at least a few legends that came to mind.

"Well, spiders factor heavily into Native American folklore. The Spider Woman is a Navajo deity that's said to be the protector of the innocent. The Spider Grandmother is believed by the Hopi Indians to be the creator of all humanity. The Inktomi is believed to be a trickster god by the Nakota Sioux tribes, the Dakotas, and the Lakotas. As far as the Cheyenne Indians go, they believe—"

Frank held up a hand, stopping her mid-sentence. Emily recoiled, realizing she'd been speaking faster than normal to keep up with the information as it flowed from her brain. When she got like that it sounded more like a tangent than a discussion, and her eyes dropped to the table. "Sorry."

He laughed and took a sip of his drink. "It's okay, I appreciate the enthusiasm. Not quite what I had in mind, though."

She frowned, wondering exactly what it was he wanted to talk about. He'd said spiders, and here they were, talking about spiders, so what was the problem?

"Mr. Tempo, why don't you just ask me the right questions if you want the right answers?"

That provoked a response, though not in the way she expected. Instead of going on the defensive like most people did when she put a little backbone into her tone, he seemed to glow proudly at her, almost as if that was the answer he'd been expecting all along.

"Okay," he said, reaching down to grab his attaché. "Have you heard of any urban legends with giant spiders in them? Legends along the same line as, say, Bigfoot, or cattle mutilations. Stuff like that."

"Bigfoot?"

"You know," he prompted, "like a story told around the campfire about a giant spider, or something like that to scare kids."

Emily instantly recalled a story she'd read about a few years ago that made her smile, but she shook it off in favor of another bite of her donut.

"What?" Frank coaxed. "Tell me."

"There was this one thing floating around the internet a while back about these giant spiders roaming wild somewhere in Missouri."

"Were they attacking people?"

"Not that I can recall. People said they were these mutations that escaped from a secret government laboratory. You know, like some weird DNA experiment gone wrong. There were even a bunch of photos to go along with it."

"Really?"

Emily nodded and pulled out her phone, tapping it a few times before handing it over. "Here, see for yourself."

Frank took the phone and removed a pair of glasses from his pocket. He put them on, and studied the images he was seeing with close scrutiny before grunting. "These things only have six legs."

"Exactly. The pictures are real, but they're not giant spiders. They're coconut crabs, the world's largest terrestrial arthropod."

A shadow seemed to pass over Frank as he looked at her and asked, "Are you sure about that?" It was enough to send a slight chill down her spine.

"Well, as far as anyone knows."

"So no giant spiders then, right?"

She shrugged. "I mean, there's been sightings of giant spiders all over North America. Wolf spiders, banana spiders, the Arizona Desert Tarantula. Those are all pretty large arachnids. How big are we talking here?"

"The size of a bathtub."

Without waiting for a response, he reached into the leather case and brought out an iPad, along with a manila envelope. He placed them on the table between them, and Emily looked on, trying to comprehend what he'd just said. She'd heard the words that came out of his mouth, but her brain wasn't processing them. Not in the way it should've. As soon as the words *as big as a bathtub* crossed his lips, she should have laughed, scoffed, or maybe even got up and left, because it was ludicrous. Spiders the size of a bathtub? Not only was it ludicrous, but from her limited knowledge of biology, it was physically impossible.

Frank slid her the manila envelope and instantly her heart started pounding. Whether it was the jolt of caffeine, the way his demeanor had suddenly shifted from relaxed to severe, or the late hour, she couldn't say the reason for her quickened pulse, but that one little gesture had been enough to turn the warm blood running through her veins into ice water.

"Have a look," he said.

She glanced out the window for a moment at their two cars side by side—hers a 2007 Chevy Cavalier she'd been unable to part with, and his a black Cadillac SUV with tinted windows and a fresh shine that gleamed under the lights in the parking lot. Something nagged at her about that, but she brushed it aside for the time being in favor of the envelope.

"I'm not going to find a picture of Rick Astley in here, am I?" she joked, trying to calm herself with humor.

"Who?"

"Never mind."

She flipped open the top flap and pulled out a set of papers. She leafed through them, seeing a police report, a witness statement, and a report from the USGS—the United States Geological Survey—about a 5.1 earthquake in West Virginia. She recalled hearing something about it on the news the other day but hadn't paid it much attention because a 5.1 wasn't all that big. Enough to cause some minor damage, but that's about it.

"What's all this?" she asked.

"Take a closer look."

She did, reading over the police report first. A man out on a hike in the mountains with his dog. An attack. The dog was abducted.

What the hell?

She read the adjacent witness statement, and kept seeing the same word over and over, "spider," along with words like "huge" and "giant."

"Clearly this has to be some sort of prank," she said, her mouth turning downwards into an annoyed frown. It always bothered her when people went to great lengths to disturb law enforcement with this nonsense. They had better things to do with their time than take reports from crackpots. The guy was probably drunk, or stoned.

Frank, as if sensing her line of thinking, reached forward and flipped the page for her. "The toxicology report shows no traces of illicit substances in his blood, or alcohol for that matter. He was stone cold sober."

"Still, he has to be mentally unstable, right? I mean, a spider the size—"

"—Of a bathtub, I know. It sounds crazy, and I thought it was, until I saw this."

He picked up the iPad and swiped it on as she set down the pages. They soaked up the condensation from her iced coffee that had leaked onto the table, but she was too focused on Frank to care. Handing her the tablet, she took it as he said, "Watch this."

Emily sat there, watching the vertical video that was obviously shot with a phone camera. It was jittery, though clearly showed the lush greens and deep browns of the West Virginia wilderness. It panned down to a golden retriever on the end of a leash, panting happily as it buried its nose in the leaves and sticks that peppered the mountainside.

Who's a good dog? A man's voice chimed. *Who's a good dog? Good boy, Buckeye, good boy.*

Buckeye the dog gruffed and kept tugging forward, evident by the strain being put on the leash.

Hang on, boy. I wanna get a look at this. God, what an amazing day outside, huh?

The video panned away from the dog and out into the wild, showing a picturesque mix of maple and oak trees set against the backdrop of a blue sky with ghostly wisps of white clouds streaming across it.

Off camera the dog barked and was hushed by the man.

The dog barked again.

Quiet, Buckeye.

Buckeye didn't shut up. His barking intensified, and the camera swung rapidly around to show him growling at something in the woods.

What is it, huh? There was no hint of urgency to the man's voice. *What's out there?*

The camera panned up just as a loud rustling gave way to the cracking of branches, and the next thing the video showed was a large shape coming into the frame followed by the man's loud screams echoing in with Buckeye's constant barking.

Holy fuck!

The video became increasingly jittery as it was obvious the man was on the run.

Jesus Christ, what the fuck was that? Panic filled his terrified question, followed by more screams of *Buckeye! Buckeye!*

He'd dropped the leash before taking off, leaving the dog behind.

A few moments later the jiggling of the frame stopped as he paused to catch his breath. Emily heard the labored breathing and the sobs before the camera panned in the direction he'd run from, showing exactly what it was that the dog was barking at.

Off in the distance, a spider crawled frantically over the canine, wrapping it in thick webbing. Its bulbous hindquarters were facing the camera, but there was no doubt as to what it was.

Eight legs.

Segmented body.

"Jesus Christ," Emily whispered in unison with the man taking the video.

She jumped back as the spider whirled around to face the camera, and for a second the video zoomed in, becoming out of focus in the process.

I'm sorry, Buckeye.

It panned away, the man started running again, and the screen went black.

Emily watched it again.

She watched it a third time.

By the fourth, it felt like someone had poured a bucket of ice over her skin and her mouth was filled with cotton balls. There were no words in the English language to describe what she was experiencing. Awe came close, so did dread, and so did fascination because if you stripped everything away, she was still an explorer at heart—the same girl who used to dig for dinosaur bones in the backyard when she was four—and this was the discovery of a lifetime.

She stopped the video and handed the iPad wordlessly back to Frank. Her gaze met his and they locked onto one another for a long while, sitting in a silence that could only be described as bewildering.

The ice melting in her cup shifted, clanking together enough to break the moment wide open. Emily blinked and cleared her throat, taking a sip of the coffee in the hopes that it would bring some of the moisture back to her mouth.

Her thoughts ran fast and furious, colliding into one another only to break apart and form new ones that scattered everywhere like shattered glass on a concrete floor. She couldn't zero in on anything coherent, not enough to speak, so she looked away from Frank and out the window again at their two vehicles.

Her Chevy.

His Cadillac SUV.

Black.

Tinted windows.

The video. The police report. The report from the USGS.

Her mind wandered briefly to her father, and all the years he'd spent drinking and terrorizing Emily and her mother. His alcoholism was a disease—a terrible, unforgivable disease—that started when he returned from Afghanistan where he served as a ranger with the 75th Regiment.

I'm an old friend of your father's.

The military, the SUV, access to official reports.

Government.

Frank Tempo was a fed.

She looked back at him, feeling her chest tighten ever so slightly at the realization as she wondered just what exactly it was she'd walked into.

Finally, she found her voice, and this time it was her turn to ask the right question.

"Who the hell are you?"

CHAPTER 3

Frank kept his gaze trained on her as he gathered up the damp reports and placed them back in the manila envelope. He took the iPad and stuffed everything into the leather attaché, asking, "You're a smart girl. Who do you think I am?"

In her travels she'd often come into contact with people who claimed to have experiences with secret government agents that didn't identify themselves as being from any one organization. Men who, in the case of a UFO sighting, or perhaps in the face of a pseudoscientific discovery, would use their presence to intimidate witnesses into recanting their statements, or scientists from halting otherwise important work that could lead to a shift in how we see the world.

Tesla was said to be the victim of men like these. The theory goes that the official reports of him dying in the Hotel New Yorker in 1943 were tampered with to make it seem like he died from coronary thrombosis, when in reality he was murdered because of his recent discovery of the so called "death ray," a weapon that could have huge ramifications on the raging Second World War if it fell into the wrong hands. He was killed, and all his scientific papers were absconded with, never to be seen again.

That was the conspiracy theory anyway, but Emily hadn't really given it much credence, or any other story she'd come across about the supposed MIBs, until now. Her mind swirled with stories she'd heard over the years dealing with everything from JFK, to Roswell, New Mexico, and though one of these men seemed to be staring her straight in the eyes, she didn't want to believe it.

"I don't know," she whispered, giving a slight shake of her head. "I just don't know."

Frank kept his thin lips tightly shut, tapping the table with a finger as he sized her up and down, though his eyes never left her face. It felt like he was burrowing his way into her soul, searching for something. Tugging at her subconscious in order to jar loose a visceral reaction she didn't know was in her.

He leaned forward and laced his fingers together, saying, "I'm just a person, Emily, much like yourself, who believes that not everything in this world is as it seems. But unlike you, I've been put in a somewhat high ranking position of power so I can actually do something about it."

"What do you mean, *do something about it?*"

"As you know our current administration has certain tendencies to brush off scientific fact, but what you don't know—nor does anyone else—is that it does have a keen interest in things of a more fringe nature."

"Holy shit."

"More important, however, is that there are some who deem these things a threat to national security, so I've been given the task of making sure occurrences like the one I've shown you are isolated incidents, and will in no way pose a problem for the American people."

"You're telling me our president believes that Bigfoot might be a terrorist?"

Frank shrugged, refusing to answer one way or the other.

Emily ran her palms down the side of her face, feeling the weight of his words. She knew the incoming administration had its issues, but this? This was a whole new level of crazy, taking her back to stories of the Nazi's searching all over the world for occult artifacts that could help with their rise to power, like in Raiders of the Lost Ark. It was almost as ludicrous as a spider the size of a bathtub.

Not so ludicrous anymore, is it?

She rolled her eyes at the stray thought as it made its way through her mind. Finishing her iced coffee, she placed the cup off to the side and turned her attention back to Frank.

"So where do I fit in all this?"

"You fit very nicely in the center, Emily. I'm building a team of people to investigate these matters, and I'd like you to lead it, starting with this business in the mountains."

"Why me?"

"Isn't it obvious? You're top of the food chain when it comes to stuff like this, and aside from having tremendous knowledge of everything from Greek mythology to cryptids in America, you've got a good head on your shoulders. You're smart, well rounded, and most important you don't succumb to every crackpot theory that makes its way onto the internet."

"I don't know, Mr. Tempo, this all seems pretty crackpot as it is."

"I'm giving you a chance, Emily, to find out once and for all what's really out there, with the backing of the United States government. Imagine what you could do, what you could find out, given unlimited resources and access to some of the brightest minds our country has to offer."

When he put it like that, it did seem pretty appealing. For years she'd toiled away with her books and investigative research, but it never felt like it amounted to much. Not once had she ever come away with definitive proof of anything's existence, and though it didn't feel like the things she did were a complete waste of time, some days it felt like if she never found the answers she sought, then what was the point in continuing to ask questions?

A far cry from what she'd told young Sophia Núñez back in the library, but it's always easier to dish the advice than take it, especially when you'd been at it for as many years as she'd been and come up with nothing but an empty plate.

"Who else is on this team?" she asked.

"I can't tell you that unless you say yes. For security reasons, of course."

"Of course." She sighed. The adrenaline that was in her bloodstream dissipated, and the night was catching up to her. She felt it in her sore eyes, her sore bones, and in her sore brain that hadn't received this much of a workout in a long time.

Maybe that's what I need.

"I can see you're hesitant," Frank said, "and that's okay. You're not the only one. When I was first asked to head this little organization, I thought it was nothing more than a way for them to put me out to pasture. I've served my country for a lot of years, Emily, but I've never been shy at voicing my opinions. When you get to be my age, and as much of a pain in the ass as I can be, you can't help but think something like this is just a token assignment. Something to get me out of Washington and everybody's hair."

"And you don't think it is?"

"No, not anymore. After speaking with others and seeing that they were dead serious about investigating these matters, I came to realize quite the opposite, that my years of experience were the reason they chose me, and your years of experience and knowledge are why I'm choosing you."

"You know I'm only thirty-three, right?"

"Thirty-three with the maturity of someone way beyond her years, Emily. Don't sell yourself short."

"And you know I have no military background, right? That was all Dad."

"I know, and we've got that covered. What I need is someone like you to guide the men and women of this team in the right direction, and help them to keep their wits about them. Without a good leader, it all falls apart, and before you know it, Bigfoot's walking into a mosque with a bomb strapped to his chest."

A slight grin crept up the side of Frank's face, and Emily tried not to follow suit, but it was all just too much, and she found herself laughing harder than she felt she had any right to. A secret organization, a giant spider in the mountains…it was like something out of a bad B-movie, but there it was, all laid out for her like a meal at a fine restaurant—all she had to do was take a seat at the table.

"Tell you what," she said. "There's a comfortable bed waiting for me at the Comfort Inn, so I'm going to go get some sleep, but tomorrow when I wake up if you have a car waiting for me, then we'll give this a trial run, okay? I'd like to at least get a feel for what I'm agreeing to before I say yes. I'll go into the mountains, meet the team, and we'll go from there."

"I think that sounds fair," Frank said. He reached into the attaché case and brought out another envelope, handing it to her.

"What's this?"

"Just a little light reading. I'll see you tomorrow morning, Emily."

Before she could ask anymore questions, he got up and left, and she watched his SUV pull out of the parking lot before tearing into the envelope, pulling out several dossiers on what she could only assume were the other members of her team.

A military captain, his two-man squad, a biologist, and a computer information technologist.

She had no idea how those were all going to fit together, but if Frank Tempo was organizing things then she'd just have to trust his judgment.

Tomorrow. She'd trust his judgment tomorrow. Right now all she wanted to do was rest, and by the time she checked into her room and made her way to the bed, her eyelids were the heaviest they'd felt in a long time.

Soon she was fast asleep, dreaming of Bigfoot riding on the back of a giant spider.

CHAPTER 4

The spider carried Buckeye deep below the surface of the earth. It brought him there, where darkness reigned supreme, and for eons the creature had lived in caverns and caves, crevices and holes, never once seeing the light of day.

Until now.

It was used to shifts in its lair. Tectonic plates crashing against one another to block off a cavern and form a new one that it could explore. It had lived like that its entire life. A life that spanned time and space, defying the odds and the natural order of things. It survived when it shouldn't have, flourished when it should have floundered. Yet there it was, with a fresh new kill. With something it had yet to experience.

The creature scurried along, its eight legs trampling the earth below, sending rocks and dirt cascading ahead of it down the slope. Its two fangs clacked excitedly together, making a chattering sound as it continued along the path laid out before it. A path that widened every hundred feet or so, leading to an opening that took it into an immense cavern that opened up ten miles below the surface. Inside that cavern was its home, along with many other spiders just like it.

Buckeye was laid out before them, and they gathered around the cocooned canine, eager to get a taste of it. They clustered together, each the same size as the spider that brought back this magnificent feast. They took turns sinking their fangs into it, careful to leave enough succulent juices for the next in line so that it might have a sample of this new meat. This went on for two minutes, maybe an hour. Time was meaningless down there.

When each of them had their turn, they backed away from Buckeye's corpse, forming a makeshift wall that protected another opening in the cavern. It was one of their two purposes in life. Guard the hole, and find the food. The guarding they did well. The finding of food was more of a challenge because deep beneath the surface there wasn't much sustenance, though they gladly gave up their lives for the one who reigned supreme over all of them. The one that birthed them.

Their mother.

She came forward, awakened by the sudden excitement that this new meal had brought. Her legs inched out of the den she called home, and the spiders guarding her parted, giving her the room she needed to roam freely. Her eight eyes scanned them all, able to see in the darkness as if it were broad daylight, a trait she'd passed on to each and every one of her babies. Finally, her sight landed on the dog, and she moved toward it, intrigued by not only its size, but also the aroma wafting up toward the hair on her legs she used to sniff the air.

Her fangs sunk into the meat, piercing Buckeye's hindquarters. They searched and probed, moving past the muscle until they reached the small intestine. The taste was incredible. Unlike anything she'd ever had the pleasure of suckling on, and eventually she finished off the dog, leaving behind a dry husk that she kicked behind her.

Her fangs clacked once, twice, three times, and the spider that brought this unusual feast to her came forward, lowering itself to the ground in supplication as its mother lifted her two front legs and reached out to delicately stroke her baby.

They had no vocal chords.

They couldn't speak.

But it was obvious to them all what mother was telling them.

More.

Must find more.

And with that the smaller spider raised itself up, turned, and headed back toward the surface where the latest shift in its lair had opened up a crevice that led to an entire world they'd yet to explore.

Behind him, his brothers and sisters followed.

CHAPTER 5

The morning brought with it a gray sky and a complimentary breakfast of watery scrambled eggs and something that loosely resembled hash browns. Emily choked it all back, promising herself she'd stop at Dunkin' on the way out of town for something a little more substantial. When she got outside, there was a black SUV waiting for her along with a driver dressed in a dark suit and sunglasses, even though it was hot and overcast.

"That isn't the official uniform of the job, is it?" she asked, injecting a bit of humor to calm her otherwise shaky nerves.

"No, ma'am," the guy said flatly.

He held open the door for her as she got in back, and when she asked if they could stop for iced coffee, he simply nodded once and closed the door.

After a quick run past the drive-thru, the vehicle made its way onto US-50, heading east, and Emily sat back with her briefcase by her side, which contained her items from yesterday, as well as the envelope Frank had given her the night before.

"Where's Mr. Tempo?" she asked.

"We've been instructed to go on ahead. He'll be in touch."

She checked her watch. It was just past eight in the morning. The drive would take a little over three hours, so she pulled out the dossiers she'd been given, studying as much as she could over the long haul.

The town they were heading to was called Franklin, located somewhere in Pendleton County, West Virginia. With an elevation of 2,222 feet and a population just under 700, its claim to fame was a summer festival held every year at the end of July, which attracted people from neighboring counties. Aside from that, it was a simple place, with simple people. A fire had devastated almost everything in the 1920s, leveling the business district, and from the ashes grew few storefronts, a small library, a bank, and a church. Most residents traveled down the mountain each day for their livelihood, working in Pocahontas and Augusta counties.

It was about as country as country could get, and deep within the wilds of West Virginia it was prime breeding ground for a legend to be birthed, though Emily knew what she was going to investigate wasn't a tall tale. Not if that video she'd seen was authentic. She still had her doubts, but they were few and far between given the discussion she'd had with Frank. He seemed dead set on taking this seriously, and if that was any indication as to what she was walking into, it was going to be one hell of an interesting day.

Flipping over to the dossiers for her team, she read up on Captain Lee "Titan" Davies, a 6'4" behemoth that Frank had plucked from the 1st Special Forces Operational Detachment-Delta, otherwise known as Delta Force.

"He's not messing around," she murmured, gazing over the decorated history of Davies, which included two medals of honor, a Distinguished Service Cross, and a Silver Star. She questioned the military presence if all they were doing was a preliminary investigation, but when she thought about how what they were up against might be real, then it was better to be safe than sorry, because sorry could mean finding yourself trapped in a giant spider's web.

She shuddered at the thought before reading up on the biologist, a woman named Michelle Liu. MIT graduate, tons of awards and honors, and her specialty was, of course, arachnology—the scientific study of spiders.

No surprise there, Emily thought.

If these were the type of people Frank had access to, then there was no telling how far his reach stretched. When he'd told her she'd have access to unlimited resources she thought it was just a passing phrase, but now it was becoming glaringly apparent that he'd meant what he said.

It was the CIT guy that threw her, though. John Collett. He hadn't graduated from an ivy league school, he had no achievements worth mentioning, and based on the photograph accompanying his file, he was just a kid of no more than twenty or twenty-one. On the surface he seemed like just a regular I.T. guy that Frank grabbed on his way out the door because his Windows drivers needed updating, but from years of experience Emily knew it was pointless to make assumptions based on speculation.

Especially if she was getting herself mixed up in a clandestine organization like this.

God, it still seemed so absurd to her, and when she stopped to think about it—really give it some thought—it blew her mind to the point where it made her question everything she'd learned, not because she wondered if it was false, but because she wondered how much more ahead of the curve she'd be if she took the time to actually believe all those crazy conspiracy theories she'd read about and listened to in her career. How many of them were true? All? Some?

She laughed to herself, setting aside the files and running a hand through her deep red hair. Huffing out a deep breath, Emily resigned herself to doing the best she could, despite not having any leadership experience in this sort of situation. Sure, she'd led seminars and spoken in front of thousands of people in her time, but this was unlike anything she'd tackled.

Trial by fire.

She sipped her iced coffee, watching the trees turn lush and full the further they got into the wilderness. The air became cleaner away from the cities, and as the vehicle took the incline up the mountain towards Franklin, it felt like everything she'd done in life was in some way preparing her for this moment. She steeled her nerves and clutched her briefcase tight, casting aside her fears and self-doubt as best she could, ready to go to work.

The driver brought the SUV to a stop just outside the sign welcoming visitors to town, which was nothing more than a piece of plywood painted a chestnut brown, the words stenciled on in yellow. He opened the door for Emily and she got out to gaze upon what she could only assume was command central, a large RV painted black that loomed over the entrance to the town as if watching everything that went on.

The driver took a cell phone out of his pocket and handed it to her. "From Mr. Tempo," he said.

Just as she took it, the device started to ring.

"Hello?" she said hesitantly.

"Good morning, Miss Nite."

"Mr. Tempo. I was expecting to see you here."

"I'm sorry, I've been detained for the moment on business, but I will be there. In the meantime, you'll find everything you need inside the Bus."

"The Bus?"

"I'm assuming you've seen the big vehicle outside Franklin?"

"Yes, I'm looking at it now. It's quite impressive."

"That's the Bus. As of right now, that is our base of operations. We thought it best to be mobile for the time being, but that could change in the future. For now, it'll have to do. Like I said, everything you need is inside. This cell phone is your direct line to me. If you should have any questions, or need anything further, don't hesitate to use it."

"I have a lot of questions, actually."

"And I'll be happy to answer them for you, but the clock is ticking, Miss Nite. We need to get moving on this situation before it materializes into something more."

"I understand."

"I knew you would. Good luck, Emi—"

"Mr. Tempo?"

There was a pregnant pause on the other end of the line as she interrupted him. Finally he answered, "Yes?"

"You sure you picked the right girl for the job?"

"I'm sure I picked the right person for the job. Good luck."

And with that he was gone. Her lifeline tying her to the men and women inside the Bus was cut off, and everything was riding on her shoulders now.

She watched the SUV drive off, swallowed hard, and turned to make her way toward the Bus. Just as she got within arm's reach of the door, it flew open and a tall, lanky boy came flying out, landing on his ass at her feet. He was quickly followed by a large, black man who covered her in shade as he blocked out the sun. The look on his face was anything but welcoming as he pointed toward the boy at her feet, who she recognized as John Collett, her computer specialist.

"Next time you wanna do something like that you make sure you have my permission first, boy. Got it?"

Emily watched Collett scramble to his feet and dust himself off. To his credit, he got right in the other man's face and started to protest, just as the two were separated by Lee "Titan" Davies, who was even taller and bigger than the black man that'd thrown John on his ass.

"Break it up, lugs," he commanded. His voice was deep and assertive, and he wasted no time getting in between the two to diffuse what looked to be a ticking time bomb of a situation.

"He started it," Collett whined.

"I don't care who started what," Davies growled, looking from him to the other man. "When you're on this team, you'll be respectful of your squad mates, got it?"

"Who appointed you leader?"

Emily cleared her throat, interjecting herself into the discussion. "I did."

Everyone turned to see her standing there as if she hadn't been before. She took a step toward them, used to being overlooked, and firmly established her dominance in the best way she knew how: by raising her voice.

"What the hell is going on here?"

Davies blinked, and Collett swiped the spittle from his chin. Emily's chest heaved up and down. Her breath felt short at the adrenaline pumping through her veins, and for a second it caused her vision to blur, but she quickly managed to grab hold of herself and stiffen her spine.

The Delta Force captain stepped forward. He was dressed in a mix of brown and green camouflage BDUs, his hair was cropped short, and his jowls were covered in a hearty brown beard peppered with strands of grey. His dark eyes fixed on Emily, who was absolutely dwarfed next to him. "Who are you?"

For a moment images of her father flashed in her mind, taking her back to when she was just a young teenager. There was a brief flicker of fear in her eyes, and she almost took a step back from the hardened military man.

Almost.

"Emily Nite," she snapped. "I've been instructed by Mr. Tempo to—"

"Hold on a second," John Collett interrupted. He raced forward and stood next to Davies. "I thought I recognized you." He reached out, grabbed her hand without asking, and started shaking it. "It's an honor to meet you. I'm a big fan."

"You…you are?" Emily cocked her head to the side, glancing from him to the captain. Looking at Collett standing next to Davies, it wasn't hard to see where the bigger man got his Titan call sign from. He was a giant.

"Sure, who isn't? I've read all your books, and when I open up my browser your website is the first thing I see. Wow, this is so cool."

She'd never met anyone who'd been starstruck by her before, so she had to work hard to suppress a smile, but there was no denying she felt flattered by the attention.

"You were saying." Lee tossed Collett an annoyed glance.

Emily snapped herself back into the moment and the job she was there to do. "Mr. Tempo has instructed me to oversee this operation, so I'd appreciate a little civility from everyone."

"Civility?" called the black man who'd thrown Collett on his ass. Emily recognized him as Earl "Oral" Plaisier from the dossiers she'd read. He bounded down the steps of the RV, shaking his head. "Ma'am, if you're looking for civilization it's about thirty miles down the mountain. Up here, all you're going to get is rednecks and Pabst."

"Not civilization," Collett groaned. "Civility. You know, being polite to one another?"

"Fuck you, geek."

"Hey!" shouted Emily. "There'll be none of that."

"Stow that shit, Oral," Titan added. "Back inside, now."

Earl looked at the ground, apologizing quietly before making his way back on the Bus.

Collett beamed proudly at her, but his expression quickly dropped when Emily said, "You too. Inside."

"So you're the boss, huh?" Titan asked, folding his arms across his broad chest.

Emily waited until everyone was inside and the door was shut tight before inhaling and exhaling a much needed deep breath.

Titan's firmly fixed gaze cracked a little, and the corner of his mouth curled up into a knowing grin. "Shit, you have no idea what you're doing, do you?"

"Not even a little," she admitted.

"It's okay, that's why I'm here."

"What do you mean?"

"The Conductor and I go way back, so he gave me a little of the 4-1-1 on you."

"The Conductor?"

"Tempo. That's what I call him since he's the boss of this whole thing, but make no mistake about it, Miss Nite, when he's not around, you're in charge, and you've got to shimmy into the role fast or else that crew in there will drive you apeshit."

"How am I doing so far?"

"I don't know, it's only been a minute, but you seem to have a spine, so that's something at least."

"Good."

She surveyed their surroundings for the first time, getting a decent look at the entrance to town, which was just a country road surrounded on either side by brush and tall trees that stretched to the sky, giving her an isolated feeling she wasn't comfortable with considering the circumstances. It felt like someone—or something—was watching them.

"You really think there's a giant spider out there?" Titan asked.

"I don't know," she whispered, worried that if she spoke too loudly the something that might be out there could hear her. "I guess we'll find out."

"Indeed we will. Come on, I'll introduce you to the others so we can put Operation Crazy Eights into full effect."

"Crazy Eights?"

"You got a better name for it?"

She shook her head. "No, I guess not."

Emily followed Titan onto the Bus, glancing back over her shoulder to look out at the vast wilderness before them, unable to shake the feeling that there was more out there than just trees.

CHAPTER 6

The inside of the Bus was unlike anything she'd ever seen before. While Emily's idea of a posh RV was something with a couch and a big screen TV, this went way beyond her expectations, completely gutting them and building from the ground up.

Gone was anything that even remotely resembled a living space. It was like someone had hollowed out the massive construct and replaced its usual comforts with an interior that resembled NASA control center.

The right wall was covered in computer screens, telephones, radar monitors, and as many keyboards as she had fingers. The left wall was partially covered in weapons that were arranged from largest to smallest—everything from automatic rifles to hand guns—while further down were shelves containing clips, magazines, and boxes of spare ammo, along with hand-to-hand necessities such as Bowie knives and expandable steel batons. It was a regular smorgasbord of everything a geek and grunt could ask for, and the crew seemed right at home.

"Welcome," Collett said. He sat closest to her, tapping away at a keyboard while on one of the monitors patterns and diagrams shifted in high definition. "Sorry about earlier," he apologized. "I get a little jazzed when someone tells me I can't do something. Maybe I took it a little too far."

"What do you mean?" she asked.

He motioned over his shoulder, where Earl "Oral" Plaisier was sitting with his FN SCAR H, stroking the barrel with a white shammy as if it weren't already clean enough. "He told me there was no way in hell I could access his personal banking information because the password was *so secure*." Collett emphasized that last bit with air quotes.

"And?"

"And I was in and out within five minutes."

"You can do stuff like that?"

"I can do anything with a computer," he smirked.

"So if he dared you to do it and you did, what's the problem?"

He shifted uncomfortably in his seat, like he didn't want to tell her.

"John?" she urged. "What did you do?"

"I may have subscribed him to a year of Pornhub Premium."

Emily tried to keep a straight face, but the partially ashamed, partially amused look on Colletts was just too much. He looked like a cross between a child caught with his hand in the cookie jar, and someone who just told you they scored perfect on their SATs.

She laughed, patted him on the shoulder, and leaned over to whisper, "Do something like that again and you'll be getting off faster than a boy scout in a whore house. Got it?"

He blushed but nodded his affirmative as Titan, who'd been listening in on their little exchange, howled with laughter, catching the eyes of everyone in the RV.

Further down the line, Emily met her biologist, Michelle Liu, for the first time. The Asian-American woman stood to greet her, and Emily had to look up to meet her gaze.

"Is everyone around here taller than me?" she remarked.

"Ma'am." Michelle offered her hand. "It's a pleasure to meet you. Don't worry about Hackman over there, I'll do my best to keep him in line."

"Hackman?"

Liu nodded. "We've given each other little nicknames."

"Ain't nothing little about Titan," Titan said.

"He's Hackman, and I'm Charlotte, like from Charlotte's Web."

"Seems fitting," Emily mused. "What about me?"

Michelle's eyes darted up and to the left, like she was thinking about it, but after a moment she shrugged and said, "I'm not sure."

"Alright, listen up," Titan boomed. "Our illustrious leader here needs a call sign. Anybody got a suggestion?"

A woman stepped forward from the other side of Earl, and Emily gave a sigh of relief when she saw someone she was finally eye-level with. Her name was Maria Lopez, call sign Hazelnut, and though the two were the same height, that's where the similarities stopped. Her olive skin and jet black hair were in stark contrast to Emily's paleness and red locks, and her build was not unlike that of a power lifter, though Emily wasn't sure if that was all natural or because of the BDUs she wore, giving her a little extra bulk. She guessed it didn't matter much; she was just glad the soldier was on her side.

"Ma'am," Hazelnut said with a nod. "Welcome to the team. You ever have a nickname before?"

Emily thought about it. She'd been teased a lot as a kid because of her looks, and though names like Red Sonja and Matchstick came to mind, she didn't want to say them out loud because of the negative connotations they held for her.

"No." She shook her head. "Never."

"How about Cryptkeeper," Hackman shouted from the front of the Bus. "You know, since she's a cryptozoologist?"

Everyone nodded their approval, with Earl piping in, "That's the first useful thing you've said all day."

"Okay," Emily said. "So just to make sure I got this straight. Collett is Hackman, Michelle is Charlotte, you're Titan," she pointed to Davies, then added, "and over there is Hazelnut, and Oral."

"You got it," Oral said.

She looked at Earl for a moment, puzzled. "Why do they call you Oral?"

"Because his last name," Hazelnut said. "It's spelled different, but it's pronounced 'pleasure.'"

Oral shrugged. "What can I say, I like oral."

The team had a good laugh over that one, Emily included.

Though she carried herself somewhat straight-laced and professional when she was out on a speaking engagement, or at a book signing, her sense of humor was a mix of dry sarcasm blended with something out of an Eddie Murphy comedy routine. She could give and take with the best of them, but now that they'd all broken the ice getting to know one another on the surface, she clapped her hands together and was ready to get down to business.

"Okay, gang, show me what you got so far."

At her command, everyone burst into action, returning to their respective stations, and her knee-jerk reaction was to flinch at the sudden flash of activity, but then she remembered that she was the one in charge. She'd have to get used to people actually doing what she said.

"I've been monitoring seismic activity in the area," Hackman said. "There've been a few slight tremors since the 5.1, but the USGS isn't predicting anything beyond that on the horizon."

"Do we think the quake had something to do with our mystery spider making an appearance?"

"Seems as good a theory as any right now. Since there was no sign of this thing before the shake, rattle, and roll, there is a slight possibility that wherever it was hiding was jarred loose by a shift in the tectonic plates."

"That's good for now. Keep on that until we know for sure where it came from. What else you got?"

Hackman slid his chair over to another terminal, pulling up an array of web browsers and going to work on the keyboard. "I've also been monitoring social media activity from pretty much everyone in town, making sure this all stays on the down low as per Mr. Tempo's orders. So far, so good. Nothing's gotten out about our little eight-legged freak."

"Good. The last thing we need is a bunch of attention being drawn to this. Nice work."

She patted him on the shoulder and turned her attention to Charlotte, who was hunched over a terminal. As Emily approached, she straightened up with a smile on her face.

"Can I just say how exciting it is to be working on something like this? I mean, a discovery of this magnitude could change the course of science as we know it."

Emily admired the woman's enthusiasm. It wasn't the initial reaction she had after learning of a spider big enough to waltz away with a golden retriever, but after the shock and awe had worn off, as a cryptozoologist she had to admit that it was pretty fascinating.

"Agreed," she nodded, "but do we know how this happened? From what I understand the physiology of a spider doesn't allow it to get this big, so what's the deal?"

"You're right," Charlotte nodded. She sat back down and pulled up a bunch of information containing spider diagrams and facts about arachnids. "The two biggest reasons spiders don't grow to ginormous sizes are their respiratory system and their exoskeleton. Like us, they breathe in oxygen and exhale carbon dioxide. The biggest difference is that their lungs depend on diffusion through these teeny tiny openings, which is much slower than our breathing system. Basically what all that means is that they don't get as much oxygen as we do, preventing them from growing any bigger.

"As for the exoskeleton, well it goes without saying that the bigger a creature gets, the heavier their exoskeleton becomes, so for a spider of this size to exist, it means that either nature found a way, or there's something else going on."

"What do you think?" Emily asked.

"I'm not sure yet. I won't know for certain until I have a specimen to deal with, but judging from the video we've all seen—" Her fingers raced across the keyboard and the same video Mr. Tempo had shown Emily popped up, paused just as the spider was whirling around to face the camera. "—I'm guessing this isn't your garden-variety spider we're dealing with. See there." She pointed to the blurry image of the spider frozen in a moment, and though it was difficult to decipher what they were seeing, it was still clear enough for them to all know what it was. "This thing has all the qualifications to be considered an arachnid, what with it having eight legs and everything, but its body appears to be different than anything I've ever seen. It's not segmented like the spider's we're used to."

Emily squinted, trying to make the blurred image come into focus. It was pointless, but she saw enough to agree with Charlotte's findings. The two main parts of a spider were the abdomen and the cephalothorax, which gave it that figure eight shape. This creature was made up of a singular body, from which its legs extended.

"Interesting, right?" the biologist asked.

"Very," Emily mumbled, still studying the image. She could've sworn at first glance she saw the normal, segmented body of a spider, but that must've been what her eyes wanted her to see because that's what they were used to. She'd have to keep that in mind in case anything else tried to play tricks on her.

"If it bleeds, we can kill it, right?" Titan asked.

Emily turned and nodded. "I'd think so, yeah."

"Kill it?" Charlotte gasped. "Why would you want to kill it? We have to capture this thing alive, Captain. For science."

"Shit," Oral groaned. "Here we go."

"Here we go what?" she snapped, bolting upright from her terminal. "You can't seriously want to kill something like this, not when we don't know anything about it."

"I don't care one way or the other, Miss Science. I'm just saying that this is straight out of every monster movie I've ever seen, okay? The science dudes want to keep the monster alive for science, and what happens? All hell breaks loose and grunts like us are brought in to clean up your mess. So yeah, here we go. I knew this was gonna happen, man."

"This isn't a monster movie, Oral. This is—"

"No?" he rushed over and jabbed a finger at the screen that had the paused image of the spider on it. "Take a good look, Charlotte, because it sure as hell looks like one to me. We got a giant frickin' spider out there that eats dogs and probably wants to eat us. If that isn't a monster then I don't know what is."

Titan leaned over, whispering to Emily, "You gonna say something?"

She gave him a firm dose of side-eye. "You started it."

The big man sighed, allowing Charlotte and Oral to go on arguing for a few more seconds before he put his fingers to his mouth, giving a whistle loud enough to rattle everyone's eardrums. That shut them up real fast.

"Put a cork in it, you two. Nobody's killing anything yet. Shit, we don't even know if that thing's still out there, or if it's even real."

"What are you talking about?" Charlotte chided. "Of course it's real. Haven't you watched the video?"

Titan nodded. "Sure, I've seen it. I've seen Sharknado, too."

"What are you talking about?"

Emily stepped forward and said, "I think what Titan means is that seeing is believing, and until one of us gets a look at this thing in the flesh it's best to consider all the options."

"Yeah, something like that. Who's to say this isn't some CGI bullshit, and we're not all on the receiving end of some viral video crap."

"Based on my analysis," Hackman offered, "I'd say there's about a 99.9—"

"—Percent chance I'm going to kick your ass if you don't let the captain finish," Oral growled.

"Okay, okay, enough." Emily held up her hands, deciding now was as good a time as any to start offering solutions before things got too far out of hand. She'd just reined everybody in, the last thing she needed was to lose control again. "We're just getting started here, so what we need to do is put a plan into action."

"Agreed," Titan said.

"So what's the plan?" Hazelnut asked. She'd been watching everyone from the corner, not giving an opinion one way or the other.

"Charlotte, you said you needed a specimen to know exactly what we're dealing with, right?"

The biologist nodded. "Yes."

"Okay, so Titan, you take your crew out into the woods where this video was shot and see what you can't find. Maybe we'll get lucky and this thing left behind some trace evidence we can examine. In the meantime, Charlotte and I will go talk to Mr. Perry and size him up. See if this all checks out."

"What do you want me to do?" Hackman quizzed.

Emily turned toward him. "Stay here. I need to you keep monitoring communications in and out of the town, as well as keep up to date with the USGS. We don't want to be caught off guard with another quake, big or small."

"Can do," he said.

Titan walked over to a cabinet on the wall and took out a small box. He passed it around to his team, with each of them picking something out of it. When Hazelnut was the last to choose, she brought it over to Emily.

"What's this?"

"Bluetooth comms, courtesy of Mr. Tempo."

"They're already set up," Titan added. "Just plug and play."

Emily grabbed one from the box, holding the device up to examine it. It didn't look like any Bluetooth earpiece she'd ever seen. It was the size of one of the earbuds on her headphones, only without the cord to get in the way. She placed it in her ear canal, impressed with how snug it fit.

"Just tap it once to turn on after you're out in the field, and we'll all be able to stay in touch," Hackman said.

Charlotte took one as well, and Titan placed the box back in the cabinet.

"Okay, gang, suit up."

He and his team got their gear at the ready as Emily and Michelle busied themselves collecting what they'd need to go speak with Mr. Perry.

When they had all prepped, she paused at the door, looking back over everyone. They stood there, waiting expectantly for her to either move or say something. Her palms were sweaty with the expectation of things to come, and she swallowed her fears as best she could. She knew they'd never be completely gone, but that was okay. Fear was good. It kept you alert, and Emily had to be alert if she was going to command this group.

"Cryptkeeper?" Titan murmured. "You okay?"

"Yeah," she said. "I'm good. I just…" Her voice trailed off. She felt like she should speak a word of encouragement to everyone. No—she *had* to speak a word of encouragement. It's what good leaders did. At least that's what she thought they should do.

"I know most of you aren't used to taking orders from someone like me, but we're all in this together now, so no matter what happens, I hope you'll all keep your wits about you, and trust that I want to do what's best for this team, and this town. We don't know what's out there yet. All this could be over in an hour, or we could be here for a while. This is new for all of us. I just want everyone to work together. To do the best we can. I'm going to mess up, but I hope you'll all bear with me and help me do my job, so I can help you do yours."

Her words were met with silence. Titan, Hazelnut, and Oral glanced at one another, and Emily thought about how stupid she must look standing before them. A well-oiled machine that'd been through thick and thin together, and here she was, trying to act like their superior when really it felt like they should be the ones telling her what to do.

But Mr. Tempo had called on her for a reason, so that had to mean something to them.

It did to her.

Titan stepped forward, his commanding presence towering over everybody. He stood next to her and together they looked at this motley crew for a moment before he placed a comfortable elbow on her shoulder.

"You heard the woman. She's in charge, so we're all gonna listen and do what she says, and if anybody has a problem with that, they can take it up with me. Now let's get out there and catch us some bugs."

Hazelnut and Oral slapped hands, shouting "Hooah" in unison with one another before heading outside. Titan clapped them on the back as they went, followed by Charlotte, who looked to be as cozy as anyone in the company of the military vets.

"My dad was in the Navy," she commented. "Hooah!"

"That's the spirit," Titan laughed.

Emily held him up at the door with a quick "Thank you" to show her appreciation.

"Just keep doing what you're doing, and you'll be okay."

She nodded, and stepped out into the unknown.

CHAPTER 7

The spider could sense something was close. It had a different scent than that of the animal it previously encountered, but it was enticing nonetheless.

It came upon a clearing in the trees, looking to and fro for a place it could set its trap before realizing that the entire ground was perfect for what it had in mind. For centuries upon centuries it hunted, always in the same way. While the modern equivalent of its species weaved elaborate webs that hung in plain sight, this spider went to work laying its silk on the ground so that anything wandering its way would be ignorant to its presence.

It shifted left, then right, laying silk less than half an inch thick across the grass. Though thin, it was still strong enough to capture an avalanche of boulders should they fall from on high. When the spider was done, it moved toward the center of the web, balanced by the fibrous hairs on the tips of its legs that barely made contact with the silk, allowing it to not get stuck in its own trap. The spider gathered leaves and twigs, as many as it could, to mask its cage to unsuspecting prey, leaving enough space for it to still get stuck upon its arrival.

Then it bent its powerful legs, and in one leap jumped high into the trees, staying perfectly still and watching. Waiting. The scent became stronger, more pronounced. Its heart rate quickened, and as much as it wanted to click its fangs together out of sheer excitement, it resisted, knowing the noise would alert others to its position.

Looking downward, the spider saw two smaller creatures break through the trees and come upon the clearing. They were dark like it was, but they only had four legs and two eyes. It saw them lumber toward the center of its trap, traipsing over the debris it had set down as camouflage. For a moment it thought they might make it all the way across, avoiding the silk entirely, and it braced itself to jump upon them and attack.

Then one of the creatures got stuck, and when the other came over to investigate what the problem was, it too became trapped. Tiny, frustrated cries of help went into the air. They wiggled and stamped their feet, causing more silk to entwine them, further sealing their fate.

The spider looked on, anticipating how good they'd taste. If they were anything like how they smelled, they would be a delectable feast for everyone, especially Mother. It moved forward, preparing to leap down on the two animals, but then something else caught its attention. It was the scent of another creature. Several creatures, in fact, and it gave pause until it was sure that it could handle this new threat.

It rested in the trees.

Continuing to watch.

Continuing to wait.

Ready to attack.

CHAPTER 8

Lee "Titan" Davies had spent the bulk of his career with Delta Force, dismantling terrorist cells and taking out HVUs deemed a threat to the country he loved. He'd been everywhere from Afghanistan to Somalia, had fought under conditions of extreme heat as well as extreme cold, and in the face of terror he'd put a smile on his face and pulled the trigger. His commanding officers used to joke that his spine wasn't made of bone—it was made of titanium.

What they didn't know, what Titan never told anybody, is that he'd also spent the bulk of his time being scared shitless, but it was that fear that made him such a good soldier. Some people let fear get to them. They let it paralyze them, cripple them, and prevent them from becoming all they could be. Not him. He embraced it like an old friend, setting it a place at the dinner table.

Fear was his ally, and right now it was a white-hot river of lava coursing through his veins because if there was one thing he hated, it was spiders.

"Man, who would have thought that after all the shit we've seen, we'd end up in West Virginia, huh, Cap?" Oral remarked as the three of them made their way deeper into the woods.

It wasn't hard for Hackman to pinpoint the location of where the video they'd all seen was shot from, and after taking one of the Jeeps through town and utilizing satellite GPS, Titan and his crew had found the spot in less than twenty minutes. They were now knee deep in the wilderness, blending in with the trees and brush.

"If you squint real hard, it's like we're in Cambodia," Hazelnut said.

"Yeah, only a little less neck and a lot more red," Titan whispered. "C'mon, it's just up ahead."

The three made their way to where the creature had taken Mr. Perry's retriever, but aside from dried leaves and a small patch of fur, there was no sign of anything left behind.

"What do you think, Oral?"

He shimmied his way between Titan and Hazelnut, glancing down at the fur, and then his eyes followed a path leading deeper into the woods. He was an expert tracker, and in his day he'd been able to pick up on the smallest of trace evidence that to anyone else would just seem like background noise, but after studying the spot and the surrounding area, he came up empty.

"Nothing, Cap. Not a goddamn thing."

Titan knew well enough not to ask for anything else. If Oral said he couldn't follow a trail, then there was no trail to be followed. Period. He'd been with these two long enough to know them better than they knew themselves.

"What now?" Hazelnut asked.

Titan surveyed the landscape. The idea of walking into something unknown didn't bother him—hell, it was part of the job—but in this case there was a twinge of uncertainty nipping at his heels. They'd dealt with a lot of enemies over the years, but all of them were human.

This? This was some crazy ass shit.

"Let's go find this thing." He pointed ahead to where the path led through the trees. "Game faces on," he added.

Hazelnut and Oral nodded once, their expressions turning rigid and fierce, and as Titan led the way up the mountain, the fear intensified, keeping him alert and on point.

Spiders, man. Giant spiders. It was unheard of, but when Mr. Tempo approached him to be a part of this mission, he couldn't resist. It seemed like a vacation compared to what he'd been used to, and though the idea of an oversized arachnid creeped him out, there was something inside of him that got excited when he'd seen that video. His whole life Titan had been interested in things that sat on the fringes of our world. Things that science dismissed, and religion hailed as blasphemous. But he knew. Deep down, he knew. The natural world was just too comfortable. There had to be more to it than what'd been explained.

This was his chance to find out. He just hated that it came by way of a spider.

He held up a fist, signaling the others to stop. He trained his ears on nature, listening for something. Anything. A rustle in the trees, the crack of a branch, the sound of something rummaging around in the leaves, but there was nothing. Just the ambient noise of birds chirping in the midday heat.

He spread his fingers and the group crouched, moving silently forward. Titan didn't have to look over his shoulder to know they were there. He trusted Oral and Hazelnut with his life. Trusted that they had his back, just like he had theirs. It's why he wanted them with him. Why, when Mr. Tempo had given him his pick of soldiers to bring along with him on this mission, he didn't even flinch.

Earl Plaisier.

Maria Lopez.

They were more than just soldiers. More than squad mates. They were family, and you didn't leave family behind. Especially when given an opportunity like this. They'd worked hard keeping America safe—protecting her interests—but this was the first time they'd ever gotten the chance to protect her on native soil.

Against a giant fucking spider, he thought. *Jesus Christ.*

When he'd told them what they were up against they didn't ask questions. Didn't scoff or say he was batshit crazy. They knew by the tone of his voice and the look in his eye that Titan was far from nuts, and what he'd said was gospel. All Oral and Hazelnut asked was *when do we get started?*

That right there...that was the definition of family.

After forty-five minutes though, it felt like Titan and his family were on a wild goose chase. There'd been no sign of anything other than a rabbit and a couple of squirrels darting between trees. The creature they were looking for was either gone, or never existed in the first place. At this point, Titan didn't know what to believe. Not until he heard one way or the other from Emily.

"What do you think, Cap?" Hazelnut asked, bringing up the rear.

The three grouped together, and Titan wiped the beads of sweat from his upper lip with the back of his hand. "I don't know," he answered honestly.

Oral started to ask, "Do you think—"

Then he was interrupted by a high-pitched wailing coming from somewhere ahead of them, and all three raised the barrel of their rifle toward the unexpected noise.

Questions aside, they quickened the pace, weaving through the trees as the sound of whatever the hell that was grew louder with each step. Titan's finger rested along his trigger guard, ready to take quick aim and fire if need be. The idea of keeping the spider alive intrigued him, but not enough to risk his life, or anybody else's.

A few paces later they broke through the trees and brush, coming upon a clearing roughly thirty-feet in diameter. In the middle of it were two struggling black bear cubs that looked to be trapped in…something.

"What the hell?" Oral breathed.

Hazelnut took a step forward and her foot came down on something that didn't quite feel like the earth she'd been used to trampling on. Titan followed her gaze toward her combat boot, as did Oral, and when she lifted it up the sole brought with it something sticky and wet, not unlike the gooey remains of a scorpion she'd once crushed in Cyprus.

They watched as the two bear cubs waddled their way around, getting caught up in the substance. It hindered their movements, trapping them the more they fought it. Their small cries for help went unanswered for the briefest of moments, until on the other side of the clearing their momma came to the rescue.

"That is one pissed off sow," Hazelnut remarked.

She was right. The mother black bear was enraged. Titan put her weight around 200-225, and when she reared herself up on her hind legs, he guessed she was anywhere between six, to six and a half feet tall. She looked at the three of them, placing blame for the entrapment of her cubs, and the guttural growl that emanated from deep within her lungs filled the air around them.

Titan raised the barrel of his weapon, taking aim just as she lumbered forward. He'd take the shot if he had to, but first he wanted to see just how sticky this stuff was.

The answer came moments later. Her back paws got caught up and she tripped, face planting to the ground. The loud growl she gave off sounded more frustrated than angry, and when she tried to raise herself upright with her front paws, the sticky goo went with her, attaching itself to her muzzle, until there was no more give and it snapped her back down to the ground. Her helpless cubs looked on, crying for their mother, desperately clawing out to her. Titan saw in her eyes a look of helpless anger as she struggled harder and harder to get to them, but it was no use, and her anger soon turned to sorrow as she realized it, too.

"This is crazy," Oral said. "What the hell is that stuff?"

Titan caught his eye. "It's silk."

"Silk?"

"From a spider."

Oral looked at him until Titan saw the realization dawn in his eyes. Whatever could produce this much webbing—this much silk—had to be huge. At least the size of a bathtub.

"What do we—"

But Hazelnut never got to finish her question. From high above them came the monstrosity they'd been hunting. It dropped down from the trees and landed between the cubs and their mother, its eight legs working frantically to secure its prey. There came from it a hissing sound that pierced through the cries of the bears, and the noise its feet made when it trampled the ground was like eight hollow drums beating all at once.

"Holy fucking shit," Oral shouted. "Look at the size of that motherfucker." He raised his barrel but Titan secured it with a tight fist.

"Hang on," he said.

Oral hung on, as did Hazelnut. Both their weapons were at the ready, and together they watched the spider completely engulf the mother bear in silk, wrapping her over and over again until she resembled a giant, struggling cocoon. Then it bit down with twelve-inch fangs that sunk deep into her flesh, and seconds later the struggling stopped. When the creature removed its mouth, Titan saw drops of paralyzing poison dribble to the ground.

Then the spider turned its attention to the cubs, but not before catching sight of the three soldiers standing before it. Pausing, the hissing grew louder. Its eight, black eyes went from the bears, to the humans, to the bears, to the humans—like it was deciding what to do next.

Titan didn't want to wait around to find out. He didn't need Emily to tell him this thing was real. Didn't need anybody to tell him anything anymore. He just needed to live, because there was no way he was getting taken out by a giant fucking spider.

In sync with Oral and Hazelnut, Titan looked down the scope of the FN SCAR. The next word out of his mouth was "Fire!" just as the spider dashed toward them.

CHAPTER 9

At about the same time Titan and his crew stumbled across the two bear cubs, Emily was knocking on the door of a Mr. David Perry.

Like the others, she'd tracked down his location using GPS, though she probably could have found him without it. Driving through Franklin with Michelle, they'd both remarked at how small it was as they passed through what they guessed was the downtown core, but really it was nothing more than a couple of blocks peppered with storefronts. A café, an antique shop, and a clothing store were the three most prominent ones to catch her eye, along with the signs pointing toward the bank and the library, both off the main drag and down side roads that led to residential areas.

Mr. Perry's address, a 21 Bleaker Street, was on the other side of town. The side that hugged the mountain close before stretching off into a wooded area that led further up toward the peak. His house wasn't a house at all, but rather a doublewide mobile home with faded yellow siding and scummy windows that made it hard to see inside.

Emily knocked again, glancing toward Michelle in the process.

"Don't think anyone's home," the biologist commented, though there was a Ford pick-up parked a few feet away from them.

"Maybe he's out for a walk?"

From inside they heard a thud, followed by a man cursing, followed by the crash of a bottle shattering, followed by more cursing.

"Mr. Perry?" Emily called out.

"Ugh," came the reply.

Michelle stepped forward and banged on the door. "Mr. Perry, we need to talk to you."

The door flung open toward the inside, and Emily stepped back, looking at the man standing before them in a pair of black boxer shorts and a blue bathrobe that looked like it hadn't been washed in centuries. Mr. Perry's hair was a sandy blonde mess of curls that went every which way but presentable, and the dark stubble on his face was a good indicator that he hadn't shaved in a few days.

His breath was an indicator that he'd been drinking those days away instead.

"Mr. Perry?" she questioned.

He squinted, eyeballing the both of them. "Who wants to know?"

"My name is Emily Nite, and this is Michelle Liu. We'd like to talk to you about what happened to your dog, Buckeye."

He stared at them, cocking his head back before asking, "You guys feds?"

They looked at one another. Emily wasn't sure how to answer that. Was she a federal employee now? She hadn't signed any documents or told Mr. Tempo one way or the other which direction she was leaning. This was supposed to be a trial run, but the further she got in knowing the men and woman under her command, the more she got used to the idea of it becoming something a little more permanent.

Michelle spoke up. "No, Mr. Perry, we're with the *Pendleton Times* and we'd really like to hear about what happened. Our readers have a right to know if something is up in these mountains."

He looked at her, swaying awkwardly from foot to foot.

Emily looked at her, too, unsure how to feel about the little white lie. They weren't reporters; not officially, though she supposed her job did entail investigative journalism, even if she wasn't attached to a formal publication.

"There's something in the mountains, all right," Mr. Perry slurred. "Fucking spider took my dog."

His face crumpled up into a mess of emotions and he choked back a drunken sob, stumbling backward a few steps before welcoming the two women into his home with an outstretched arm.

Emily went in first, instinctively putting her fingers to her nose at the pungent smell of body odor and alcohol that filled the air inside the mobile home. She glanced around the mess, noticing a laptop sitting amongst a pile of strewn out papers and open books, all of which had to do with the subject of spiders.

"You want a drink?" Mr. Perry asked, swishing his way over to the fridge.

"No, thank you," she said, watching as he twisted the cab on a bottle of Budweiser.

"Suit yourself." He guzzled half the contents and burped.

"Mr. Perry," Michelle said, "do you happen to have the phone you shot the video on?"

He mumbled something about not telling anybody about the video, but searched through the mess on his kitchen counter regardless, unplugging the device from the power cord when he'd found it.

"Here, see for yourself."

Michelle took it from him and Emily watched it all again, glancing up at Mr. Perry to see his reaction. He stared aimlessly out the dirty window, sipping from the bottle.

"Just fucking left him there like a coward," he said to himself. "Buckeye never hurt a fly unless I asked 'im to. He didn't deserve to go out like that. Damn dog was my best friend and I just left him. Who does that? Me, that's who."

"How big would you say this spider was, Mr. Perry?" Emily's tone softened a bit, sympathetic toward his feelings.

"Bigger than my dog, that's for damn sure." He looked at her, the red rings around his eyes becoming more pronounced the more they filled with tears and guilt. "I'd say at least the size of one of them bean bag chairs, maybe bigger. That was just its body, though. Can't forget about the legs. All fucking eight of them. Jesus Christ, what kind of spider was that?"

Michelle shook her head. "We don't know yet, Mr. Perry, but we're working on it. Is there anything else you can tell us about what happened?"

He wiped his nose with the palm of his hand, shaking his head. "No, not really. One second me and Buckeye were walking along having a good time, and the next thing I knew there it was, right in front of us."

"Was it coming down the mountain toward you, or up from the base?" Emily questioned.

"It was coming from up above. If it was coming from down below I'd say it was something straight outta hell, but who knows? Do demons live in heaven?"

Emily opened and closed her mouth, thinking about remarking how Satan was originally an angel, but thought better of it.

"You tell the people to stay off that mountain, you hear?" Mr. Perry pointed at them. "It ain't safe to go up there."

"Have you told anyone about what happened?"

"Told the whole damn town, but you think they believe me? Course not. I wouldn't believe me, either. Giant spider. Who the hell's gonna buy a story like that?"

"Did you show anyone the video?" Michelle asked.

He mumbled a no and took another swig of beer, peering down the neck when it was all gone, like he was checking for a few more drops.

Emily nodded toward the laptop and the mess of papers on the table. "Were you able to find out anything?"

"Huh?" Mr. Perry followed her gaze, his cheeks turning a shade redder when he saw what she was looking at. "Nah, that's just me tryin' to be clever to keep my mind off Buckeye, you know?"

"So you didn't find out what kind of spider it was that attacked your dog?" Michelle added.

He shrugged. "Found something that looks close to it."

"Can you show us?" Emily felt a twinge of hope. Maybe this visit would prove to be more fruitful than at first glance.

Mr. Perry hobbled over to the laptop and smacked the spacebar, bringing the screen to life. "Found this on the National Geographic, but like I said, it's not exactly what I saw, just close to it."

Emily leaned in, with Michelle close behind looking over her shoulder. Together they read about something called *Cryptomartus hindi*, a coin-sized spider that existed during the Carboniferous period roughly 325 million years ago. Judging by the fossil records, this spider didn't have a segmented body, just like the one they'd seen on Mr. Perry's video, but it was way too small to be the culprit.

It was *something*, though.

"What do you think?" Emily whispered.

Michelle shrugged. "I'm not sure what to think. I've heard of them before, but like Mr. Perry said, it's too small. Whatever he saw—whatever we saw in that video—it could pre-date even the *hindi*, if that's what we're dealing with."

"You saying my dog got taken by a dinosaur? Shit, you two sound crazier than I do."

Emily and Michelle both stiffened at his words, their meaning not lost on either of them.

"Taken?"

Mr. Perry nodded at Emily. "Yeah. Fucker wrapped him up in its web or whatever and carried 'im off."

"So you're saying that it didn't kill your dog?" Michelle asked.

"Not like, right away, but what else is it gonna do with him? Course it's gonna kill him."

"Most spiders consume their prey immediately, Mr. Perry, but there are some species that will wrap it up in a cocoon-like confine to consume later. They paralyze it with venom to subdue it before wrapping it in silk, thus preserving it for when it's ready to feed."

"What are you, a reporter or a spider expert?"

"Bit of both," Michelle said.

"So are you saying Buckeye could still be alive?"

Emily saw her eyes dart away, glancing toward the ground as she said no in a solemn tone.

What little hope had sprung into Mr. Perry's shoulders quickly dissipated. She felt bad for him, but better to hear the truth now than to go on thinking that there might be a chance for his friend.

"I'm going to find that fucking thing one of these days," he said through gritted teeth. "And when I do I'm gonna kill it, I promise you that."

Emily took a deep breath, seeing the anger and sadness in his eyes. There was nothing more to say. He had his mission, and she had hers, and as Mr. Tempo said: the clock was ticking. They had to find this thing before something other than a dog got attacked.

"Thank you for your time, Mr. Perry,"

She offered him a comforting pat on the shoulder before stepping outside with Michelle in tow. When the door was shut, she turned to see the biologist scratching her head.

"It just doesn't make any sense. If this spider is anything like what we saw in there, then it has to be billions of years old."

"You don't think it could be a new species?"

"No, like I told you, spiders in this day and age just don't get that big."

"So we're dealing with something prehistoric?"

"Or alien." She smirked.

But Emily wasn't laughing. She wanted answers. It was what she'd based her whole life around: finding answers. Every single time it'd felt like she'd come up short. She didn't want it to happen again. Not this time. Not with all the resources at her disposal.

They had to capture this thing alive. It was the only way either of them would know for sure.

CHAPTER 10

"Is it dead?" Oral took a step forward, looking at the spider lying motionless on the ground.

They'd each emptied their magazines, for a total of 60 rounds of 7.62x51mm NATO rimless bottleneck cartridges that shredded the creature. Six of its eight legs were curled up into itself, with the other two severed from its body, spasming like sciatic nerves. Smoke flitted on the breeze, moving up the mountain in a gray haze.

Titan lowered the barrel of his SCAR. His chest heaved and his pulse raced, and for a second he had to close his eyes and take a few deep, calming breaths. He'd remember that thing charging at them for a long time to come. Those fangs, those eyes…it was the stuff nightmares were made of.

"I think it's dead," Hazelnut said, shouldering her rifle. "It has to be. Look at it."

They did. It was a bloody mess, filled with lead and leaking bodily fluids that reeked of copper. Its blood wasn't red, but rather a dark aqua color that seeped out the open wounds, trickling to the forest floor. Its eyes were lifeless—as lifeless as the eyes of a thing that didn't blink could be, anyway.

Titan stared into their black abyss, still clutching his rifle tight against himself. He expected a jump scare, like in the movies when the protagonist creeps upon a lifeless corpse only to be scared shitless as it reaches out and grabs them. He knew that was stupid, but that's how he felt in the moment. A part of him wanted to empty another mag in the damn thing just to be sure.

"It's dead," he said, reassuring himself.

"Damn," Oral hissed. "Bet Charlotte ain't going to be too happy about that."

"Who gives a shit," Hazelnut spat. "It was him or us, man, and no way in hell it was going to be us."

Titan tapped his earbud and walked away from the two, leaving them to stare at the still-struggling bear cubs who were now without a mother.

"Cryptkeeper, this is Titan, do you read?" He waited a few moments and then said again, "Cryptkeeper, this is Titan, over."

"Cryptkeeper here. What's your status, Titan?" Emily's voice came through loud and clear.

"We found the spider."

"You did? That was fast. Are you tracking it now?"

He looked back over his shoulder. "You could say we tracked it."

"And? Where is it?"

"It's about twenty feet away from me lying in a pool of its own blood, Cryptkeeper."

He braced himself for a barrage of criticism but instead was met with silence. In a way that was worse. He heard Emily sigh, pictured her running her fingers through her hair and the look of disappointment on her face.

"Copy that, Titan."

"Sorry, boss. The thing charged us. We found it in the woods. It'd trapped some black bears and we had no choice."

"Black bears? Did you say it trapped some black bears?"

"Yeah, two cubs and their mother. Damn thing wrapped her up tighter than a Taco Bell burrito. Paralyzed her with some sort of poison."

"That checks out with Mr. Perry's story, too. He said the same thing happened to his dog, Buckeye. Black bears? Really? Those are pretty big, aren't they?"

"Big enough. Listen, this thing is still pretty solid despite being gunned down. Do you want the body?"

He listened as she talked to Michelle. Faint whispers followed by the biologist swearing. Titan smiled despite himself. Who knew the good doctor had it in her?

"We'll take it. Can you bring it back to the Bus?"

"I think we can do that." He nodded. "We got a tarp in the back of the Jeep. Should fit nicely in there."

"Okay. We'll meet you back there."

"Roger. Titan out."

He tapped his earbud to end the communication and went back to Oral and Hazelnut, who were busy cutting through the silk webbing with a pair of Ka-Bars.

"Gotta get to those cubs, man," Hazelnut said. "Set 'em loose."

"Stow it," Titan answered. "Need you to go back to the Jeep and grab the tarp. We're gonna wrap that thing up and bring it back to the Bus. I'll take over here."

Hazelnut nodded without question, sheathed her knife, and took off in a brisk jog back toward their vehicle.

Titan took up her position, kneeling next to Oral. He unsheathed his own blade and started cutting.

"Charlotte pissed?"

Titan nodded. "She's got a mouth on her like an Ohio sailor."

"Nice." Oral grinned. "I like that."

Titan eyeballed him for a second, seeing the look of mischief in his eyes. Oral always had been a bit of a ladies man, or at least he fancied himself one, but he and Titan both knew that his bark was worse than his bite, and 99.2 percent of the time Oral struck out worse than a little league batter in the majors.

"Shit," Titan laughed, drawing out the word.

They kept cutting, joking, and laughing, taking their minds off the horror they'd just faced, and when they reached the two cubs, Titan set them free, allowing them to face the big bad world alone.

CHAPTER 11

The noise was unlike anything the spider ever heard before. It was loud and abrasive, causing the hair on its body to vibrate in such a way that it couldn't help but be drawn to it.

It scurried forward, across the grass and through the trees, walking freely for the first time in its life. No longer was it confined to a chamber, or to the tunnels and caves burrowed through the earth. Its world had expanded, opened up, and it was like it was experiencing everything for the first time again, as it had upon its birth so many eons ago.

It crashed through the trees and paused, unaware that it was an alien to this new world. It felt no fear, no hesitation. All it felt was hunger, and the desire to please the one who gave it life.

Pivoting forward, it heard the noise closer now, on the other side of a barrier that it could not see through. Its movements were sharp and purposeful, and though it felt no fear it knew it had to be cautious. It was a sense it had, was born with.

It didn't know it, but the noise it heard was the voices of children on the other side of a wooden fence. There were dozens of them, celebrating the birthday of one of their friends, Tiffany Albright, who was turning nine years old. That scent it smelled was pheromones mixed with the aroma of hamburgers and hot dogs sizzling on a charcoal grill.

It didn't know it, but the spider was about to stumble upon the greatest feast of its life.

It took a step forward, sizing up the barrier. One leg balanced on it, then another, and another. Tiny setules grasped the wood grain, allowing the spider to crawl up and breach the top of the fence. It hovered there for a moment, unseen, its eight eyes seeing all. Children ran and shouted, while right on the other side of the fence a little girl and her friends were playing Pin the Tail on the Donkey.

The spider zeroed in on the girl who had the blindfold over her eyes and was aimlessly searching for something she couldn't see. It was the perfect prey. It shifted its body weight, preparing to leap, and all at once the fence gave out beneath its girth and it toppled forward. It hit the ground, holding its position, as the others saw it for the first time.

More noise erupted against it, even louder than before. It was frantic and fearful, causing chaos all over the backyard. It watched as the little children ran, being directed inside by bigger, more able adults that looked on in horror as it sat there, fixated on the one person who had yet to discover it.

Little Tiffany Albright, who was still searching for the donkey.

She moved forward, toward the spider, and it raised itself up. She jabbed it with the pin on the end of the fluffy tail, causing a shimmer of pain to shoot up its leg. The spider hissed as she peeled off her blindfold, gazing upon the monstrosity before her.

Before she could scream, it pounced, knocking her to the ground and digging its fangs into her young flesh. Paralyzing poison shot through her veins, rendering her helpless, and the spider went to work spinning her into a cocoon. Round and round it twirled the little girl, encompassing her legs, her arms, and just as it got to her neck it felt another pain shoot through its leg. It hissed once more and spun, seeing a man standing up on the porch with a shotgun in his hand. It didn't know what that was, just that it caused harm. It felt another blast hit its face, rendering one of its eyes useless. Blood gushed from the wound.

It had a thought that it could run right at the man and sever his head from his neck with one chomp of its fangs, but it already had its prey neatly secured. There was no need to stick around and feel more pain.

It grabbed hold of Tiffany with its two front legs and lifted her up, scurrying over the broken fence and back into the woods, leaving the others behind.

It would get its revenge on the man.

It would get its revenge on all of them.

CHAPTER 12

Emily stood outside the Bus next to Michelle and John, eagerly awaiting the return of the spider. As much as she would have liked to have captured it alive, she understood the position Titan and his crew were in out there in the wilderness. With something that big, something that unknown, it was impossible to tell how she'd react in their situation, and if Titan said it charged them and they had no other choice, she had to believe him.

Michelle, on the other hand, wasn't too happy. She stood with her arms folded defiantly across her chest, looking like she was ready to tear him a new one when he got back.

Emily understood her position, too, but all she could do was hope that cooler heads prevailed once they got a look at the creature.

It wasn't long before they came barreling down the road in their Ranger SOV. Typically used for light attacks and reconnaissance missions, the Jeep had been retrofitted specifically for use on native soil. Gone were the pinto mounts and rollbars that were normally used to attach machine guns and grenade launchers to, leaving more room to carry any urban anomalies the team might come across, such as a giant spider.

It ground to a halt a few feet away, the tires kicking up gravel dust. Emily, Michelle, and John both went around back as Titan whipped open the tarp to reveal the corpse of the beast.

"Holy shit," John whispered. "Look at the size of that thing."

Emily did look. She looked hard and long at it, her limbs trembling ever so slightly. It felt like every nerve ending in her body was on fire. She'd never seen anything like this. In all her years studying cryptids and different urban legends tied to folklore, there'd never been any mention of a giant spider, save for that one time in Missouri, which wasn't a spider at all. This though…this was definitely a spider, and she took a step forward to get a closer look, trying to understand the ramifications it could have not only on the scientific community, but her career.

"We need to document this," she said.

Michelle stepped up beside her and Emily took a quick glance in her direction. The look of resentment she'd displayed earlier had all but disappeared, replaced with an expression of wonder at the thing lying dead before them.

No one said anything for a long time. John ran back onto the Bus and came back with a camcorder, training it on the spider while slowly walking around the vehicle, sure to get it from ever angle. He put a soda can next to it for scale, and when he was done he picked it up and drained it of its remaining liquid before going back inside.

Finally, Michelle cleared her throat and said, "It's good you killed it."

Titan drew back, somewhat surprised.

"We don't have anything to house it in. It's going to be a chore just getting it on the Bus to study."

"Are you kidding?" Oral piped up. "I'm not riding with that thing."

"It's dead, man." Hazelnut shot him a look of annoyance.

"Yeah, but it stinks."

She shook her head as Emily stepped up to the plate.

"It's done. We're getting it on the Bus so Charlotte can do her job. Maybe she can find out what kind it is, and where it came from."

"Thought it came from that earthquake?" Titan asked.

"We don't know for sure," Emily said. "For all we know this thing could've been out there all this time."

"But why attack now?" Michelle placed her hands on her hips, not taking her eyes off the spider.

Emily shrugged. "Who knows? They're hundreds of documented cases of animals attacking urban areas that have expanded onto their turf. You have to remember, before humans started industrializing everything, this land belonged to the wildlife. Who's to say it didn't just get tired of hunting in one little area?"

"Well, regardless of where it came from," Titan said, "or why it's here, it's dead now, so Emily why don't you get Tempo on the phone and let him know, and we'll start unloading this thing to bring it inside."

Emily reached into her pocket and pulled out the cell phone she'd been given as the three military soldiers started lifting the tarp, with Michelle guiding their movements. She called up Mr. Tempo's number and was about to hit Send when John came running off the Bus, nearly tripping over himself.

"Guys, guys! We got a problem."

Everyone turned their attention toward him, and he stood there, sweat pouring off his face, which looked like it had just seen a ghost.

"What is it?" Emily asked.

"There's another one. Another spider."

"What?" Michelle hurried over, waiting for an explanation.

"Come on, listen."

He motioned for them to follow him on the Bus, and when everyone was situated around his terminal he unplugged a set of headphones from a jack, filling the space around them with a frantic voice.

9-1-1, what is your emergency?

Oh God, we need help. Something just took my baby.

Ma'am, what's your name?

Karen Albright. Please, you have to hurry.

You said someone took your child?

No, not someone. Some thing. *I don't know what it was. We were out back for Tiffany's birthday party and it just crawled over the fence.*

The woman's sobs were overwhelming, and her voice was filled with uncertainty and terror. Emily's face drained of all its color as she continued to listen to the 911 call.

Okay, Karen, what's your address?

34 Charles Street. Please hurry.

I'm dispatching a unit to your home now, Karen. Can you describe what it was that took your child?

It was big. I don't know. It looked...it looked like a spider, but I don't know.

A spider? Did you say a spider, Karen?

Yeah. I know it sounds crazy but—

Emily reached forward and killed the audio by hitting MUTE. Then she whirled on Titan, and said, "Let's go. Now. Hackman, move the Bus so it blocks off the road. There's only one way in and one way out, and the last thing we need is more eyes on this. Charlotte, get to work examining the corpse and see what you can find out. Oral, I need you to stay here. Get that thing on the Bus as fast as you can, and run interference with local law enforcement. Franklin doesn't have a police department in town, but the sheriff's office is only fifteen miles away. It won't take them long to get here, and when they do, keep them at bay."

"What do I tell them?"

"Make it up as you go along," Emily said.

"But—" Michelle started to protest.

"No buts. If there's more of these things out there and they're attacking humans, we need to stop them. Now."

"Copy that," Titan said, slapping Hazelnut on the back before the two moved into action, heading toward the back of the Bus to where the ammo was stored. He grabbed a duffle bag and loaded it up with clips, flash grenades, smoke grenades, canisters, an extra set of BDUs, and on the way back they grabbed two more rifles along with a riot gun.

Emily watched them acting like two kids in a candy store. "You sure that's enough?" She smirked.

"No," Titan said, "but it'll have to do for now. Got some stuff for you, too."

He hauled ass outside with Hazelnut right behind him. Oral was already out there dragging the spider carcass off the Jeep, making room for Titan's stash, which he promptly tossed in the back while Hazelnut got behind the wheel.

Emily took one last look at John and Michelle, offering them a firm but warm nod of appreciation, and then she climbed in back of the SOV, watching as the Bus roared to life and started blocking off the road.

CHAPTER 13

Hazelnut rounded the corner onto Charles Street and promptly slammed the breaks, bringing the SOV to a grinding halt.

"Shit," Emily mumbled.

The scene outside the Albright residence was chaotic to say the least. A crowd had gathered in front, with a line of people disappearing around back of the house leading into the yard. Most of them look pissed off, with a few confused onlookers wandering around wondering what the hell was going on. When they caught wind of Tiffany's abduction, they joined the pissed off bunch in anger.

"How do you wanna play this, boss?" Titan said, turning toward Emily who was in the back seat.

She had no idea how she wanted to play it. Nothing like this ever came up before, and she suddenly felt tight in the chest as the anxiety of the moment overtook her, blurring her vision slightly until she managed a few deep breaths, getting herself under control.

"You okay?" Hazelnut asked.

She nodded, and got out of the vehicle, noticing how quickly her teammates followed her lead.

Without saying anything, Emily made her way through the crowd, following the line toward the backyard. Most people, upon seeing Titan's girth and the firepower he was packing, were happy to get out of the way, but others scowled at the presence of the law, no doubt used to handling things their own way here in Franklin.

Emily scanned the yard; her gaze noticing the broken fence and crying children huddled with their parents for comfort. She kept looking around until she saw a man and a woman being consoled by a large group of people.

"Those must be the parents." She pointed and without waiting for confirmation from anybody, made her way over to the couple with Titan and Hazelnut following close behind.

"Mrs. Albright?" she questioned when they'd managed to break through the gathered crowd. "Mr. Albright?"

A woman's red-rimmed eyes looked up at her from the seat of a plastic lawn chair. The bags under them were puffy and pronounced, and her nose was equally as red from all the blowing. Emily noticed a ball of tissues clutched tight between thin fingers that trembled.

She kneeled down so that she was eye level with the woman, placing a sympathetic hand on her knee. When she spoke, Emily's voice was soft and understanding, even though she couldn't possibly imagine what this mother was going through. To have a child ripped from your grasp like that, and by some monster. It must've been terrifying.

"Mrs. Albright, my name is Emily Nite. We received your call about Tiffany. Can you tell us what happened?"

The woman blinked, but didn't say anything. It was her husband, a stalky man with hard calluses on his hands, who stepped forward and spoke. "You with the sheriff's department?" he asked.

Emily regarded him for a moment, deciding what to say. She didn't want to lie, but at the same time she didn't want to alarm the Albright's that the situation was direr than they could imagine—if it were possible to imagine a worse scenario than your daughter being snatched away by a giant spider.

"No," she finally said. "We're with a different organization. One that specializes in events like these. My team and I were called in by the sheriff to help find your daughter."

Mixing truth with fiction seemed as good an idea as any, she reasoned with herself, and besides, what the Albright's—what the residents of Franklin—didn't know, wouldn't hurt them.

Mr. Albright regarded her for a moment before looking to Titan and Hazelnut and the firepower they carried with them. Then he nodded once, and squeezed his wife's shoulder, as if giving her permission to speak.

"Mrs. Albright?" Emily urged. "Can you tell me what happened?"

The woman sobbed, swiping at her nose with the tissues in her hand. Her voice was shaky, but when she spoke it was with the proudness any mother might have toward their baby.

"She was over there, playing Pin the Tail on the Donkey with her friends. Jim was over at the barbecue grilling up the food, and I was on the porch tending to Donnie's scrape. He fell down and banged up his knee, so I went inside to get some Neosporin and a Band-Aid, you know, for the cut. When I came back outside I looked over at Tiffany to see how she was doing, and the next thing I knew the fence had fallen over and there was this…this…this *thing* standing there looking at her."

"What did it look like, this thing?"

Her eyes glazed over for a moment, and as much as Emily hated to have to put her through this, she needed to know exactly what happened if they were going to be able to track the spider down and rescue Tiffany, if it wasn't too late already.

Mrs. Albright's voice wavered, but she took a deep breath and continued. "I don't know what it was. I mean, I guess a part of me does, but I keep asking myself how? How can a spider get that big? It was the most god-awful thing I've ever seen. Eight hairy legs, eight eyes, and fangs…oh God, those fangs. They bit into my little girl and…" She broke, and the tears streamed down her cheeks.

Mr. Albright—Jim—placed an arm around his wife and gave her a tight squeeze. "It's okay, dear." Then he looked at Emily and finished the rest of the story. "That damn thing bit into Tiffany and she went limp right there in front of it. Paralyzed, you know? Then it started to wrap her up in a bunch of crap, and I went inside to get the double barrel. When I came back out I took a shot at it. Got the sucker right in the leg. All that did was piss it off, though, I guess. It turned around, so I took another shot, and hit it right in the eyes. Don't know how many of them I got, but that was enough to send it packing."

"And it took your daughter?"

"Picked her right up and carried her off like she was a feather. I shoulda went after it."

Mr. Albright's face burned red with anger and regret. Emily stood, and flicked a glance toward Titan.

"You did all you could, Mr. Albright," he said, stepping forward.

"Did I?"

Titan didn't have a response for that. Emily couldn't blame him. She saw how much Mr. Albright was hurting. That much was evident in his expression. He looked disgusted with himself. Like he should've done more as a father to protect his daughter.

Titan cleared his throat. "Sir, we're going to do everything we can to get your little girl back, you hear?"

Emily broke away from the group, turning her attention toward the busted fence and the last place anyone had seen Tiffany. She imagined her there with her friends, laughing and playing the way innocent young girls do. They way she'd done when she was that age, without a care in the world. That was before the bad times. Before her father became sick from the war, the way so many do when they return from seeing such horrors.

Would she end up like that? Would chasing monsters and rescuing little girls affect her in the same way serving in the military did her father? After all, isn't that what she was doing? It wasn't the Army, or the Navy, or even the Air Force, but in a way she was attached to all those things now. Working with Delta Force soldiers, Mr. Tempo, they all led back to the same place.

I took another shot, and hit it right in the eyes.

Mr. Albright's words penetrated all other thoughts, and she quickened her pace toward the fence. If he'd shot it, then there was a good possibility that it left a trail of—

"Blood," she whispered, looking down at the ground. She surveyed the carnage and followed the trail of spider blood with her eyes until it disappeared in the woods behind the house, which in turn led up the mountain. She spun, and called for Titan and Hazelnut to join her.

"What's up, boss?"

"Look."

She pointed to the blood on the ground.

"Son of a bitch," Hazelnut whispered. "It's just like the other one."

"Yeah, only this one's still alive," Titan added.

"Do you think we can track it?" Emily asked.

"We?" Titan's eyebrows shot up as he looked at Emily.

"I'm going with you," she said.

She watched him and Hazelnut exchange glances, but before she could say anything else their attention was drawn to a loud voice coming around back of the house.

"Where is it?! Where's the fucking thing that took my niece?"

Onlookers parted to allow the man through. He was big and burly, with a beard stretching down to his wide chest. He had a duffle bag slung over his shoulder, which he adjusted as he barreled his way straight for Jim and Karen Albright.

"Karen!" he called. "Karen, where is it?"

Emily murmured, "Must be the brother," as the three made their way back toward the parents.

"Sam, we'll handle this," Jim Albright told his brother-in-law.

Sam, who dwarfed the man by at least a foot, squared his shoulders and looked down at his sister, who found a fresh set of tears to wipe in the presence of her brother.

"Damn right we'll handle it," Sam said. He dropped the duffle bag on the ground, unzipped it, and began pulling out AK-47 after AK-47, handing the rifles to those who would accept them.

"Jesus Christ," Hazelnut said. "It's a fucking redneck army."

"Excuse me!" Emily yelled over the growing whoops and hollers. "Excuse me!"

Sam eyeballed her from a crouched position as he handed another rifle to a man who looked like he should be sitting behind a desk doing someone's taxes. Then he noticed Titan and Hazelnut standing next to her and stood. Stiffened, really. The way a man does when he feels threatened.

"What's going on?"

He looked down on Emily, and she clenched her jaw at the wide grin he'd developed upon seeing her.

"Well, what've we got here?"

"My name is Emily Nite, and we're here under orders from the sheriff to take care of this problem, so you can just take all those guns and put them right back where you found them, and then—"

"Found 'em? Hell, I own 'em. Every single last one. Name's Sam Falkner, owner of Shootin' Sam's."

"Lemme guess," Titan said, his deep voice low and condescending. "That's a gun shop, right?"

"Best damn one in three counties," Sam added. "Now see here, I heard about what happened to Tiffany, and no offense to you little lady, or your two G.I. Joes, but this here's a local matter. Now, we'll get her back ourselves, so you don't have to worry your pretty little head about it, okay?"

"Sam—" Karen started to protest, but was quickly hushed with a stern look from her brother.

"Karen, it's okay. That's what I'm here for. You and Jim don't gotta thank me. It's my job as an uncle to protect my niece, and that's what we're all gonna do, right?"

He turned toward the crowd and the several men who were now equipped with semi-automatic rifles. There were at least ten of them that Emily could see, and with the kind of firepower they were sporting, they grew more courageous with each passing second.

"Right?" Sam repeated.

"Right!" came a voice off to her right.

"Damn right!" another said off to her left.

More hollers, followed by men pumping their guns into the air like they were trophies.

"I don't care if it's a spider, a cockroach, or God-fucking-zilla himself, we're gonna get that little girl back, you hear?"

As everyone shouted their approval at Sam, Titan grabbed Emily and drew her away from the growing mob. She noticed that these men weren't the only one's with guns. Aside from the weapons Sam had brought, there were others in the crowd with handguns they were either holding, or had tucked into the belt of their pants.

"We gotta get this under control, boss, or else we're gonna have all kinds of trouble on our hands."

Emily stood there chewing the inside of her cheek, a nervous habit she'd developed as a child. She felt the weight of her position in that moment for the first time. How? How was she supposed to get this under control? A bunch of men with guns hell-bent on rescuing a little girl? Did she even want to get it under control? After all, it was only her, Titan, and Hazelnut out here, and while she was sure the two soldiers could handle themselves in a fight, who was to say there weren't more of those spiders out there, and what then?

Maybe a redneck army wasn't such a bad idea.

CHAPTER 14

Michelle Liu was wrists deep in the torso of the giant spider carcass when Oral asked, "How do you do that?"

She glanced over her shoulder, regarded him thoughtfully for a moment, and then answered, "I don't have a gag reflex."

Oral shifted his weight from one foot to the other, the innuendo of her statement not lost on him, or his call sign. He looked around the construct she'd erected after they'd both discovered that the Bus was too small to dissect the monstrosity in. It was nothing more than an inflatable tent that she had scrunched down to the size of a backpack. Unfastening some straps, she had pulled a cord and it blew up to the size of a small trailer, though it wasn't rectangular in shape. It was a geodesic dome, big enough for the two of them, and the dead spider, which they'd hefted onto a folding table.

"Amazing," the arachnologist whispered to herself, peering inside the open cavity.

"What's amazing?" Oral took a step forward, leaning over slightly to get a better look.

"Arachnids have two methods of breathing, book lungs or tracheae, neither of which are anything like our respiratory system. Book lungs are stacks of small plates called lamellae. The oxygen in our air passes between them, diffusing through the tissue and into the blood."

"And tracheae?"

"Tracheae are small tubes held open by rings of chitin. These tubes open to the outside of the body, allowing the spider to take in oxygen."

"Like fish gills," Oral said.

"Exactly, like fish gills."

"So what's so amazing about this thing?"

"Come see."

Oral didn't move. It's not that he hated spiders; it's just that he wasn't too keen on being close to one this big, even if it were dead. He could still see it alive and well in his mind, trampling a black bear like it was nothing. When it charged them and Titan gave the go-ahead to fire, he was the last one to pull the trigger, frozen in place for just a second while the beast closed the gap between them. He'd never frozen up like that. Ever. As far as he was concerned, the sooner they got this whole operation over with the better. Then he could go back to killing things on two legs instead of eight.

"Come on," Michelle urged. "I don't bite."

"It's not you I'm worried about," he said, taking cautious steps forward until he was beside her.

"Look," she spread open the chest cavity, revealing two sac-like organs. "Lungs, not unlike our own, and if you see here," Michelle's finger traced a small tube, "this seems to be the bronchus, indicating this creature's respiratory system is extremely similar to ours."

"What does that mean?" Oral asked, furrowing his brow.

"It means that whatever this species is, wherever it came from, it pre-dates anything known to science, because the oldest known spiders come from the Carboniferous age, which took place 359 million years ago during the Paleozoic era, and they look nothing like this."

Oral stared at her, his brain trying to comprehend what Michelle was saying. He looked from the spider, to her, and back again, shaking his head in confusion. "You lost me, doc. Are you saying this is a prehistoric spider? Like, a dinosaur?"

"I'm saying that this creature comes from deep time, a geological time, when the earth was in its infancy. When volcanos were erupting, when continents were shifting, when life itself was just beginning. It would explain why it's so big. Back then the oxygen levels in the atmosphere were the highest they've ever been, allowing things to grow exponentially larger than they are now. As the dust settled, those oxygen levels have been slowly decreasing, thus through evolution and changes in the environment, things became smaller, more manageable."

"So you're saying we evolved from spiders?"

"No, I'm saying spiders evolved from this creature. This is the very first species of spider to have ever existed. Ever. In the history of everything."

"Whoa," Oral whispered, taking a long hard look at the arachnid carcass laid out before him. He didn't pretend to be book smart; his knowledge of history and dinosaurs and evolution was formed by watching shows like Cosmos, and Planet Earth, but he was smart enough to realize the magnitude of such a discovery. He—they—were all a part of something bigger than themselves, and a creature like this could prove invaluable to understanding the early building blocks of not only life as they knew it, but also how the planet was formed.

He shook his head once more. It was a struggle to even think about it.

"You wanna see something else?" Michelle asked, clearly amused by his childlike wonder.

He shrugged. "Not like we're going anywhere."

"Help me turn it over."

Together they hefted the spider onto its belly, allowing an unhindered look at its back. Michelle knocked on it, her knuckles rapping against a hard surface.

"The reason it weighs so much is because of this hard, outer layer. Again, modern day species have nothing like it."

"Seems more like something you'd see on a crab."

"True, but it would make sense for a creature like this to have developed a harder exoskeleton if it originated when I think it did. It was a time when the world was in chaos. Mountains forming, rocks shifting and falling. It would almost have to have something like this as a defense mechanism to survive. To protect it from debris and other predators that may have been around."

Oral nodded. "At least it's not hard enough to stop bullets." He patted the butt of his SCAR for emphasis.

"No, I imagine not. Back then there would have been nothing traveling at the same speed as a projectile fired from a weapon, so there was no need to develop defenses against it."

"You know this is some pretty crazy shit, right?" Oral asked, taking a step back and straightening out. He took a deep breath and ran a hand over his crew cut.

"Don't I know it," Michelle said. "My colleagues at the ISA are never going to believe this."

"ISA?"

"International Society of Arachnology. I'm a sitting council member."

"Of course you are." Oral grinned.

Michelle rolled her eyes and turned her attention back to the spider.

Oral couldn't help but chuckle to himself. He liked this woman, even though she was infinitely smarter than him. She was more beautiful than any person he'd ever laid eyes on, and he'd laid eyes on a lot of people. She had an exotic charm to her, and while he was mulling all that over, Hackman interrupted his thoughts, breaking through on an open comm channel.

"Uh, guys, we've got company."

Oral quickly darted out of the tent and went around the Bus, peering down the road to see two vehicles fast approaching. One of them was a police cruiser, and the other was a black SUV following close behind it.

"Looks like the cavalry's arrived," Hackman said, dashing up beside him.

"Just let me do the talking," Oral told him, his grip tightening on the rifle he held close.

The police cruiser braked, kicking up road dust, and from behind the steering wheel came a tall, middle-aged man wearing aviator sunglasses. He was clean-shaven, and his hands were rough and calloused, giving way to hairy wrists that poked out from beneath a crisp brown uniform shirt. He had a commanding presence, and Oral was sure that when he walked into a room most people were impressed, but he wasn't most people.

"Sheriff Moss," the man said as he approached. He didn't extend a hand in greeting. Instead he looked past Oral at the large vehicle blocking the road, his hand resting on the butt of the glock holstered to his hip. "Wanna tell me what's going on here?"

"First Sergeant Earl Plaisier, and I'm afraid that's classified. I'm going to need you to get back in your vehicle and turn around. This area is now under the jurisdiction of the United States government." He didn't know if he was supposed to say that or not, as Emily had told him to make it up on the fly, but to him that sounded intimidating enough to rattle any small town sheriff into thinking that whatever was going on must be big. Too big for them to handle.

Unfortunately, Sheriff Moss didn't budge. He took off his shades and met Oral's gaze with a pair of ice-cold browns as he slipped them into his breast pocket. He glanced briefly at John, then back to the soldier, and Oral did his best to seem officious, while at the same time clenching his jaw shut and preparing to do what he had to in order to keep Moss at bay. If that meant using brute force, he was going to be ready.

The door to the SUV opened and Oral took a quick look to see a familiar form haul itself out onto the pavement.

Mr. Tempo.

His superior approached with no trace of alarm or worry to his posture. He walked the way a man would walk taking a stroll on the boardwalk on a Sunday afternoon. His black suit was pressed, his dark sunglasses hid his eyes, and his hands were shoved into his pockets and didn't move when he came up beside the lawman. The only indication that he'd even seen Oral came by way of a minuscule nod that was so fast if Oral had blinked in that exact moment he would've missed it.

Moss ignored Mr. Tempo's presence, and pointed a finger in his direction. "I need you to move your vehicle, First Sergeant. We've got a situation in town and it's my job to protect these people, so I don't care if you're with the government, the United Nations, or the goddamn New World Order, I'm going to do my job and there isn't—"

Mr. Tempo cleared his throat, and took Moss by the arm, saying, "Sheriff, if you'd please."

"Who in the hell are you?"

"Please," Tempo held out his hand while still keeping a firm grip on Moss's elbow. "This will only take a moment."

The sheriff looked like he was going to protest, but something in the way Tempo held on to him made his feet follow the older gentleman, and Oral watched as they walked over to the SUV. He couldn't hear what they were saying, and he took a glance at John, who seemed amused by the whole exchange. He wasn't so sure the situation warranted amusement, but to see Tempo take control the way he did caused a slight grin to form at the corner of Oral's mouth.

"What do you think he's saying?" John whispered.

Oral shook his head, not even wanting to hazard a guess as to what Mr. Tempo was telling the sheriff. A lie, a half-truth, the whole truth? It didn't matter to him, so long as when Moss came back he was willing to surrender his position.

But Sheriff Moss never returned. Instead, he got back behind the wheel of his cruiser and sped off down the mountain.

"What did you say to him?" John asked as Tempo approached, his hands still resting in his pockets.

Oral didn't know much about the man, just that he was in charge of the overall department he now found himself a part of. Titan was his direct superior, Emily was Titan's, and Mr. Tempo was Emily's. That was all First Sergeant Earl Plaisier needed to know. He'd given his entire life to others, and they'd never steered him wrong.

Hackman, on the other hand, didn't seem to have as much reverence for the chain of command as he should've.

Mr. Tempo, his sunglasses shielding his eyes, ignored the question. "Local law won't be a problem anymore. Now, bring me up to speed on what's been happening."

"Right this way, sir," Oral said before leading Mr. Tempo toward the spider carcass.

He heard John step-in behind them, little mousy footsteps trying to keep up with their long, purposeful strides. "Yeah, but what did you say?" he asked again.

Oral spun and shot him a look as if to say, *Ask that question one more time and I'll blow your head off.*

Hackman stumbled and shut his mouth.

CHAPTER 15

"How do we even know where it took her?" someone in the crowd asked.

Emily watched Sam bound up the steps and take center stage on the back porch. He held up his hand much like a politician would do, and shouted, "There's only one place it could've gone, and that's up the mountain. I say we fan out, head on up there, and the first one to find that godforsaken thing gets to hang it over his fireplace!"

She frowned and broke free of Titan and Hazelnut to make a beeline for Mrs. Albright, hoping against hope that she might be able to talk some sense into Sam.

"Please, Karen, isn't there anything you can do to stop this?"

The woman regarded Emily, her mouth forming a surprised "O." "Stop him? Why would I want to stop him? He's going to get my Tiffy back."

"Honey," Jim said, taking his wife by the shoulders while looking at Emily. "These people are professionals. If anybody can get back Tiffany, they can. I think you need to talk to Sam before someone gets hurt. I mean, Mr. Frasier's never fired a gun before in his life, now look at 'im."

They all turned their attention to the man who appeared like he should be filing their taxes. He was bald on top, with a rim of hair horseshoeing around his skull. A bit pudgy, he adjusted a pair of horn-rimmed glasses that drooped off the end of his nose with one hand, while clutching the rifle awkwardly in his other. He kept nervously glancing at it, like he was afraid it could go off at any moment even though his fat fingers were nowhere near the trigger.

Karen Albright sighed, running a tired hand down the side of her face.

"Please," Emily coaxed. "Your husband's right. These soldiers I'm with have all kinds of experience dealing with hostile situations. They will get your daughter back, Mrs. Albright, I promise."

Truth be told, she had no idea if Tiffany was even still alive, and as much as she hated to lie to the girl's mother, if it meant defusing this volatile situation then so be it. The last thing she wanted was for more innocents to get hurt, and she had a feeling if a bunch of untrained men with guns went up into those woods, that's exactly what would end up happening.

The two women locked onto one another, with Emily trying to appear understanding and sympathetic to Karen's cause at all once. She knew the woman was hurting—she would be too if it were her daughter—but she also knew the clock was ticking, and something had to be done fast so she, Titan, and Hazelnut could begin their hunt, or else who knew what might become of little Tiffany Albright.

Karen nodded, and Jim let go of his wife to allow her the space she needed to talk to her brother.

Titan nudged Emily, saying, "Good job, boss. Let's hope she can get through to him."

"I hope so."

"If not," Hazelnut said, "do we have your permission to take him out?" She patted her waistline, and Emily looked to see a baton hanging off a belt secured firmly in place.

"Let's cross that bridge when we come to it," she whispered, "but be ready, just in case."

Titan and the female soldier both nodded, and everyone expectantly looked on toward Karen and her brother, Sam, who were in a heated conversation with one another off to the side of the house.

This is it, Emily thought. *The moment of truth. Either he relents, or it's going to get messy real fast.*

She was sort of prepared for things to get messy, as much as someone like her could be. She knew Titan and Hazelnut would be able to do what needed to be done in order to subdue this situation, but she wanted to try diplomacy first. It was her way. She wasn't a fighter. She was a talker. Emily wasn't even sure she wanted to go up into those woods with her two squad mates, but she didn't really have much of a choice. Not only was she their leader, but she was also—for all intents and purposes—an explorer, and all the questions she kept asking herself begged for answers. Answers that were right there, so close. The only way she could know for sure was by getting a first hand look at one of those spiders for herself, even if it meant putting her body in harm's way.

"Here he comes," Titan murmured, and Emily snapped her mind back into place, watching as Sam stormed their way.

She folder her arms across her chest, trying to appear like she was ready for a fight, but whatever anger Sam had been displaying before looked to be dissipating thanks to the talk with his sister.

"Okay, look," he said, "I don't know who you people are, but Karen over there seems to think you know best, so I'll make a deal with you. You three can all go on your giant bug hunt, but I'm coming with you, no buts about it. She's my niece, and it's my job to make sure she's safe. Everyone else will stay behind to help keep a lookout, but I'm going, and that's all there is to it. Do we have a deal?"

Emily felt Titan and Hazelnut both stiffen, knowing full well what they had to say about Sam's proposal, but she never took her eyes off him. He was as serious as serious could get, and internally she had to tell herself this wasn't a battle she could win, not without force, and tensions were already running high. Who was to say if Titan and Hazelnut made a move on Mr. Falkner it wouldn't draw the ire of the rest of the crowd? A crowd that could easily train their weapons on the very people who were trying to protect it.

"You have yourself a deal," Emily told him, "but you follow my lead. What I say goes. If you have any issues being told what to do by a woman, I suggest you get that off your chest right now."

Sam stared at her, and she braced herself for a slew of expletives, but none came. His face softened and he broke into laughter that slowly increased the further it lasted.

"Hell," he choked out, "I'm a married man. I'm used to being told what to do by a woman." He followed it up with a slap on his thigh before doubling over as what remained of his laughter coughed out a set of smoker's lungs.

"Fine," Emily said, "then it's settled." She turned to Titan and Hazelnut, saying, "Meet your new squad mate."

They both groaned, and Hazelnut looked for sure like she was going to say something in protest, but just as she opened her mouth the words were covered with a fit of screaming that came from somewhere. The whole crowd turned their attention toward it, and Emily quickly picked it out as coming from around front of the house.

"Now what?"

"No idea," Titan said, "but we better see what's going on."

The screams were alarming at first, as most screams usually are, but the louder they got, the more terrifying they became. No longer were they screams of surprise, or even screams of warning. They were screams of terror—screams of pain—and soon they were joined by others that rained down on the residents of Franklin like a giant hailstorm.

When Emily rounded the corner and Charles Street came into view, she stopped dead in her tracks, seeing for the first time what all the screaming was about.

"Jesus, Mary, and Joseph," Hazelnut made the sign of the cross over her chest as Titan raised his FN SCAR, ready to fire at not one, not two, but a multitude of giant spiders that had descended upon the town like locusts, attacking everything in sight.

Bodies lay in the street being ripped to shreds by giant fangs that oozed venom. Spiders occupied rooftops, the tops of cars, and the beds of trucks. Emily watched one crash through the window of a house and grab hold of an elderly woman who'd been rocking back and forth in a chair, her back facing the street. The spider smashed the picture window with ease and took hold of her—chair and all—dragging the surprised grandmother into her yard. She didn't even have time to scream before the creature sunk its fangs into her wrinkled face, in essence obliterating it into a bloody mess that resembled the ground beef Emily bought at the grocery store.

Severed arms, legs, and heads flew into the air, landing and rolling with dull thuds as they hit the ground. The carnage was unlike anything any of them had ever seen. These people were nothing more than food for the giant beasts, which filled not only their central vision, but peripheral as well. They'd come out of nowhere, and were now everywhere, laying waste to the picturesque neighborhood. Perhaps even beyond. No one could be certain. All they could hope for was to stop this onslaught before it was too late for Franklin and the entire state of West Virginia.

Hazelnut reacted first, taking aim with her SCAR before firing into a group of spiders that were hovering over the carcass of a man and his dog. She sprayed their bodies with bullets, sending them flying back against a house. Two of them were shredded in seconds, with another two scrambling forward with five of their eight legs still intact.

Titan joined her in the fray, firing with his weapon to finish the job, and the spiders soon fell into bloody heaps of prehistoric flesh that twitched and leaked fluid all over the pavement.

Emily backed away, allowing those with firearms to step into her spot to do all they could to ward off this barbarous display. She knew most species of arachnids never attack unless provoked, but these…these were on an entirely different level. Never before had the world seen anything like it, and if they didn't manage to stop it, they wouldn't have to worry about seeing it again because there would be no one left to witness it.

Yet through it all, the only thing she found her mind focusing on to remain sane was Tiffany Albright, the little girl who'd been abducted. It was the only thing she could do to stay calm, otherwise she'd be driven mad at the sight of these monstrosities ripping bodies limb from limb. This wasn't her field. She wasn't a soldier, and she sure as shit had never stepped foot in any war zone, though she supposed she didn't have to. One had just been dropped right at her feet.

She had to deal.

She raced forward and grabbed Titan right after he'd shredded another spider before it could sink its fangs into a little boy that'd been knocked off his tricycle. He spun, facing her with a mixture of determination and fear in his eyes.

"We have to go after Tiffany," she screamed over the constant barrage of gunfire.

He looked over his shoulder, then back at Emily. She stood stout, firm in her determination to at least try and find the abducted girl.

"What about these people?" Titan shouted.

Emily's eyes frantically searched for a way out, scanning the thralls of people who were standing their ground, doing everything they could do fend off the spiders. As she looked, she saw one of the beasts smash the hood of an oncoming car with one of its heavy legs, stopping the vehicle dead in its tracks. Someone fired at it through the windshield, hitting it in one of its black eyes, but all that did was anger the creature. It jumped, bringing down its two front legs through what remained of the glass barrier, caving in the man's chest and sending a fountain of blood spewing forth from his mouth.

"Get Sam to stay," she shouted, catching sight of the redneck not ten feet away from them.

Upon hearing his name, he turned and yelled, "I'm going after my niece!"

Emily clenched her teeth, seemingly in a no-win situation. If they all stayed, Tiffany was probably dead, but if they left, there would be a mass grave to fill upon returning to what was left of Franklin.

"I'll do it," someone called from behind her. "I'll stay."

Hazelnut. Her voice was like a symphony breaking through the jackhammering sound of bullets flying everywhere.

Titan took a shot at a wayward spider in between kills, and ran over to his squad mate, clasping a thick hand on her shoulder. "Are you sure?" he asked. "You don't have to do this."

"Yes, I do," she said. "You go—I'll hold things down here. Just make sure you make it back alive."

"Same goes for you, soldier."

"Thank you," Emily added. "We'll stay in constant communication with one another. If things go south, you let us know and we'll come back for you."

Hazelnut took a look around them. "With all due respect, ma'am, I'd say things are way past south already and heading straight for hell."

Sam ran over to the group, shoving his hand into his pocket. He fished around for a set of keys, and handed them to Hazelnut. "Here, these are they keys to my shop. It's over on Kline. If you can make it there, you'll find all the firepower you need to take out these bastards. There's also a whole bunch more guns in the back of my truck over there, so hand 'em out all you want."

She snatched them from his grip, securing them in one of the pockets of her BDUs.

Emily regarded her for a moment, wanting to say something about how brave and courageous she was, perhaps leave her with a few words of encouragement, but when Hazelnut caught her staring, she simply nodded once and yelled, "Go!" in Emily's face, sending everyone into action.

"Come on," Titan yelled. "Let's grab some extra gear out of the SOV and we'll head up the mountain. We'll leave the mags and grenades for Nut, and then we're gone."

"Okay, I'll radio the Bus and let them know what's going on. Hopefully they're not in the same position we are."

"What do you want me to do?" Sam asked, bringing up the rear.

They both turned, and in unison said, "Kill anything with eight legs."

Sam grinned and started shooting, protecting Emily and Titan as they rushed toward the SOV to get suited up.

CHAPTER 16

After seeing the spider carcass and hearing Michelle's theory as to its origins, Mr. Tempo followed Hackman back onto the Bus, leaned over his shoulder as the young computer technician took his seat, and said, "Show me what you got."

Anyone else would have been beside themselves upon seeing what Tempo'd just seen, but he took it all in stride. After watching countless times the video of Buckeye getting attacked, there was no doubt in his mind that something was in the West Virginia wilderness, and seeing it laid out before him just confirmed what he already knew. It didn't matter that it was huge, it didn't even matter to him that it was dead. All that mattered was stopping more of them from getting loose and doing damage.

"Okay, so I've been keeping up with the USGS and so far so good. There's been no traces of any aftershocks in the area. A few tiny tremors, but they've been barely detectible. If we're talking Richter scale, then you're looking at a .0000000001. Very miniscule."

"Perfect," Tempo said. "What else? What's been happening on social media?"

"So far, nothing." Hackman hit a button and instantly the four computer screens on the wall before him switched to Facebook, Instagram, Twitter, and YouTube. "Everything's been quiet, but I am ready to intercept anything that goes through."

"And how do you plan on doing that?"

"I've ghosted every single account registered in the area, so if someone posts something it will appear to them like it's going out online, when really the information is being directed to a secure server."

"What about when no one comments on their post? I know if I posted something about a giant spider online, I'd expect at least one person to say something, no?"

Hackman nodded. "I've taken care of that, too. By accessing the accounts, that also gives me access to information regarding people's friends, followers, whatever, so if they post something, I can act like I'm one of their friends and respond to it accordingly, either by liking what they post, or commenting something along the lines of 'holy shit, that's crazy.' The original user will see those comments appear, and the accounts I'm posting under will have no idea about the content that was posted. It's all very Cloak and Dagger."

"Impressive," Mr. Tempo said, and it was. In his position he knew the government had access to technology beyond what the public thought of as current, and now that access was at his disposal, but to see it being put to use first hand by Hackman was a true example of just how far ahead of the curve the United States was compared to the rest of the world.

"Also," John continued, "I know I'm not a scientist like Miss Liu, but I've taken the liberty of looking up some more information in regard to our eight-legged friend outside, and I've come across what's know as the *Mongolarachne jurassic*, the oldest known spider in the world. It's the largest known fossil of a spider, dating back 165 million years. I don't if that helps any, but I thought I'd bring it up, just in case."

Mr. Tempo nodded. He appreciated the kid's gumption, but even he already knew that information. No, what they had outside definitely predated anything you could find online, or in any sort of archeological history book. If Michelle Liu said they were dealing with what was perhaps the very first species of spider, then he had to believe her. That woman knew her stuff, though he suspected once they got the carcass back to a more suitable examination facility they'd know more in time.

Still, he patted Hackman on the shoulder. "That's good work, John. Keep me abreast of any new develop—"

"Look, something's just been posted," he interrupted, pointing to a Facebook alert that'd popped up on one of the screens. He clicked on it, bringing the post front and center, and blinked. "What the?" Hackman whispered.

It was a video, but from the still-shot it was hard to make out exactly what they were seeing. Tempo reached forward and clicked play, and at first it was difficult to decipher as the images bounced around from a shaky cell phone, but when they steadied, there was no mistaking what the two of them were watching.

Spiders.

"Holy crap." John bolted upright in his chair, his spine stiffening. "Is that what I think it is?"

Mr. Tempo nodded but said nothing. He was too busy watching one of the monstrosities tear into the carcass of something that used to look human. Used to. Now it looked like nothing more than a rotting piece of meat someone had left on the side of the road.

"Where is this?" he asked, his voice clipped and firm.

"Uh…" Hackman leaned forward, punched some keys, and said, "Right here in town. Charles Street. That's where Emily is."

"Get her on the comm, now."

John nodded and reached to open up a channel with Emily, but before his finger could touch the button, her voice crackled through the speakers on the Bus.

Hello, is anyone hearing this? This is Cryptkeeper, over? Hackman, are you there?

"Cryptkeeper, this is Hackman, I'm here with Conductor, what's your status?"

Are you seeing what we're seeing?

"Affirmative. We have video coming through now. Looks pretty bad."

It's worse. Titan and I are going after the little girl that was abducted. Hazelnut's staying behind to help keep things steady. She sure could use some backup.

Mr. Tempo listened intently to Emily's words. There was a certain confidence in her tone that told him her nerves were under control, and for right now that would have to be enough. He couldn't expect her to do much else given the circumstances, but as long as she and her team had a plan, he knew that would at least give her a north star to latch onto and help guide the way.

"Cryptkeeper, this is Conductor. We're sending Oral in with backup." He motioned for Hackman to jump outside and bring in the rest of the team. John did as he was asked, scrambling into motion, and when he was outside Mr. Tempo asked, "Do you have a twenty on the lair yet?"

No, not yet, but we think these things might've been jarred loose by the earthquake a few days ago. We're going to keep a lookout as we search for the girl. With any luck we'll find it and be able to seal it off.

"Negative, Cryptkeeper," he replied. "I need you to do more than just seal it off. You and your team have to go in there and put a stop to these things at the source."

There was a brief pause before Emily responded, *Say again?*

"The source, Cryptkeeper. Find the source."

We'll do our best, sir.

"Good luck."

And with that Mr. Tempo cut the channel as Oral and Michelle joined Hackman on the Bus. He whirled on them, pointing to the soldier. "Bring all the firepower you can carry into town. Take the SUV outside. Hazelnut will be waiting for you."

"What about us?" Michelle asked.

"We'll hold down the fort. I'll keep at the ready in case any of them find their way here, but for now it looks like they're pretty set on getting as much food as they can in town. We might see a straggler or two, but I'll take care of it. For now, your jobs are still the same. Hackman will keep securing social media, and Doctor Liu will continue her examination."

"These things go down pretty easy if you pump them full of lead," Oral told him.

"Noted," Mr. Tempo said. "Now hurry, from the sound of it Hazelnut could really use your help."

"Done." Oral brushed past him to grab the biggest arsenal he could gather.

Tempo watched as everyone sprung into action. It'd been a long time since he'd been out in the field, and even when he had been, he'd never faced a threat like this. Up until now the enemy had always been human. Two legs, two arms, and a throat that could be cut. Now it was like something out of science fiction.

Even though he knew there were things in this universe that couldn't be explained, it didn't make it any easier going up against the unknown in a fight he wasn't sure they could win.

He turned his attention back to the computer screens where the Facebook video was still playing on a loop. He watched the giant spider tear apart flesh and bone with fangs the size of his forearms. A chill went down his spine—the first since they'd begun this mission—and he whispered, "God help us," to himself, hoping that someone up there was listening.

CHAPTER 17

Emily's choice of clothing when out in the field chasing cryptids was jeans and a sweatshirt, so for her to be draped in a battle dress uniform felt awkward to say the least.

After a quick trip back to the SOV, she'd suited up in the extra pair of BDUs stuffed in the duffle bag, while Titan filled her pockets with extra magazines, grenades, and strapped a baton to her waist, making sure to leave plenty behind for Hazelnut should she need it.

"Do you know how to shoot a gun?" he'd asked.

She'd nodded, though when he handed her a rifle it wasn't what she had in mind. As a young girl her father had taken her out shooting with a 9mm, but that was the extent of her gun knowledge, and it'd been so long ago that she was sure anything she remembered about the experience was wrong.

"It packs a punch," Titan told her, "so be careful of the recoil."

She thought about saying something but didn't want to waste anymore time. When the moment came, she knew enough to point the barrel at the target and pull the trigger. All she could do was hope for the best. It was all any of them could do.

Now, with the ringing of gunfire behind them, she , Titan, and Sam followed the trail of blood left behind by the injured spider Jim Albright had dinged before it escaped with his daughter. Droplets of the creature's blue plasma peppered the ground, left behind on leaves and grass that snaked a trail up the mountainside.

Titan led the way, with Emily in the middle, and Sam bringing up the rear. The rifle felt awkward in her grasp, and the outfit she wore was hot, causing droplets of sweat to run down her ribcage.

"How do you wear these things all the time?" she asked.

"You get used to it," Titan said.

She rubbed her side, trying to soak up as much moisture as she could. There were worse things in the world, she imagined.

Yeah, like getting your face chewed off by a giant spider.

She'd done her best to not think about what was happening back in town, but it was hard to shut that part of her brain off. Those sights and sounds were now embedded in her memory for the rest of her life, and try as she might not to think about them, it just made them that much harder to block out. It's like when someone tells you not to think of a specific thing, like an elephant. Of course that's all you're going to be able to think about. It's human nature, though that didn't stop her from trying to forget.

"You guys do this a lot?" Sam asked from behind.

Without turning, Titan said, "Oh, sure. All the time. Last week we fought off a raging group of penguins up north."

"Really?"

Emily choked back a giggle, glad for the momentary distraction from her thoughts. "No," she said, "not really."

"So what are you, some sort of special-ops team or something?"

"Something like that," she said.

"All hush-hush right? Like Men in Black?"

"Yeah, you're lucky we haven't killed you yet," Titan added, chancing a severe look over his shoulder.

Sam's footsteps faltered, and though she hadn't known him that long, Emily could tell that there was a twinge of honesty to her partners' words. She knew he didn't approve of Mr. Falkner coming along with them, but under the circumstances and pressure she was facing, it was their best course of action for the time being.

"Hey, I'm just trying to help," he said in response.

"Thank you, Sam. We appreciate it," Emily interjected before an argument developed.

Titan shut his mouth as she suppressed a grin.

Boys will be boys, she thought, wondering if her father had ever been that way. Maybe in his early days of service, but after coming back from the Middle East time after time, he wasn't the same man she remembered. When she stopped to think about it, which wasn't very often these days if at all, she could see the progression in his moods. He hadn't said much after the first tour, though he eventually returned to normal. The second time he was worse—easily agitated; and upon his third return from oversees he was a completely different person. Hitting the bottle—and her mother—hard. Gone were the days of digging in the dirt for dinosaur bones and being taken on field trips out into the wilderness.

The man she knew was gone, and as Emily stared at the back of Titan while he led the way up the mountain, she couldn't even begin to fathom how his time in the military had changed him over the years. He seemed to have a level head on his shoulders, but as she knew from experience, people had many faces. The one he wore now wasn't necessarily the same one he wore in private.

As long as they figured out a way to stop this threat at the source, though, he could wear any face he wanted to if it got the job done.

A rustling in the brush up ahead brought Emily back into the moment, though she'd never truly been gone from it. Her brain had a way of multitasking various thoughts while she worked, but after hearing something suspicious it was now trained on one thing: staying alive.

Titan held up his fist, indicating for them to stop. Sam, having no military training that they knew of, didn't know the signal and ended up crashing into her from behind. Before he could protest, she spun and cupped a hand over his mouth while placing a single finger over her lips. His surprised eyes stayed confused until his brain registered what she meant. *Be quiet.* He nodded in understanding and she removed her palm.

Titan inched his way forward, rifle at the ready. Emily tightened her grip on her own weapon, hoping against hope she didn't have to use it. The rustling noise increased, becoming progressively louder the closer they came. Her heart pounded and her breath quickened. She wasn't ready for this. Not yet. Not ever. Yesterday she was lecturing a group of students, now she was trying to save people's lives. It made no sense to her how she'd found herself in this position. It didn't seem fair. It was like asking the president to fly the space shuttle. Not that she was dumb, not that the president was dumb, it's just she felt completely out of her element, and this moment proved it.

"Oh God," she whispered, watching Titan stretch out his arm. His hand latched onto the tip of a branch.

He looked back over his shoulder to make sure her and Sam were ready, though all she could manage in response was a set of raised eyebrows and a screwed up face.

Titan quickly peeled back the bushes, sending two jackrabbits dashing between his legs. Emily cried out, nearly leaping out of her combat boots in surprise.

Sam started laughing. "Shit, ain't nothing but a couple of fuck bunnies."

Titan didn't say anything. He didn't acknowledge his comment at all. His gaze was still trained on the bushes.

Emily, noticing his lack of response, asked, "Titan? You okay?"

"Mr. Falkner, what was your niece wearing when she was abducted?"

Sam scratched his temple. "I'm not sure. I wasn't there when it happened, but if I know that girl, and I do, I'd hazard a guess that she was wearing her yellow Spongebob t-shirt and a pair of blue jeans. Why?"

Titan turned, holding a piece of yellow fabric in his hand. Emily took it, examining it closely before saying, "See this seam here, it looks like it might be from a shirt collar. That goes with what Karen said, that Tiffany was only wrapped up to her neck. It's possible a piece of her shirt got caught on a branch and tore away."

"Then she might still be alive?" Sam asked.

Emily looked into his eyes, seeing the hope in them. Far be it for her to take that away from him.

"Yes," she said. "I think so."

"Come on, we better keep moving," Titan said, making his way forward.

Emily kept her mind and eyes trained on her surroundings. She pushed thoughts of her father, of the absurdity of her leading a mission like this—all of it—out of her head. When she started to wonder what might be happening back in town, she grit her teeth together so hard it felt like they might shatter, but it was enough to stop the wandering thought from settling in and making itself at home. Tiffany was all that mattered right now. She had to stay focused on her.

"Look, there's another piece," Sam said, pointing off to the right.

They looked, and sure enough the trail of blood they'd been following veered of course, leading to another fragment of cloth dangling from a stray bush. Sam ran to it, even though Emily tried to reach out her hand and stop him.

"Sam," she called out in protest.

"Oh my God," he said. "Holy shit."

She exchanged a quick glance with Titan and they jogged over to where he was standing. He wasn't looking at the piece of cloth, or the bush. His eyes were trained on something beyond it, on the ground. Emily stepped around him to get a better look, and gasped.

"Tiffany!"

"Stay back," Titan hollered, holding up his SCAR and stepping in front of the both of them.

Lying on the ground up ahead was the body of Tiffany Albright, wrapped up in spider silk, her eyes closed and her face pale.

Next to her was the spider that'd taken the little girl from her birthday party. Its body was a bloody mess, caught within the steel jaws of an illegal bear trap that someone had set up on the mountainside. Its legs were twitching and it hissed the closer Titan came to it.

"It's still alive," Emily called out sharply, though it was obvious to everyone that yes, the spider was still breathing.

"Not for long," Titan said.

He walked over to the beast, placed the barrel of his rifle against its face next to where Jim's shot had connected, and pulled the trigger. The semi-automatic quickly snuffed out what little life remained in its battered body, and the spider fell limp within the trap.

Sam ran over to his niece, dropping his weapon and falling to his knees. When his hands touched her body they came back away from her with the sticky silk still attached to them in giant strings that he tried to fling away and wipe free on the ground. "God, what is this shit?" he asked.

"It's webbing," Emily said.

Titan took out his knife, grabbed hold of a bunch of the silk, and started slicing. "This'll take care of it," he said, making long, sharp cuts down the middle of Tiffany's torso, careful not to cut her in the process.

"Is she still alive?" Sam asked.

Emily avoided the spider's carcass and came upon the other side of the little girl. When Titan had freed her chest enough, she placed a delicate hand on her breast and waited to feel some indication that the girl still had life in her. It was faint, but it was there.

Emily nodded. "She's good, but I don't know for how long. Sam, you have to get her to a hospital. Now."

He glanced at her, then at Titan. "What about you two?"

"We have to keep going," she said. "You'll need to carry her back yourself, and do everything you can to avoid what's happening down there. There are vehicles waiting near the entrance to town that can take her to a hospital. Can you do that?"

"I'll do whatever it takes to save her," he said, reaching down to scoop her into his arms. "You two be safe, ya hear?"

"Thank you, now hurry."

"Here," Titan said, picking up Sam's AK-47 off the ground. He slung it over the man's shoulder where it dangled at his back. "Just in case."

He didn't say anything, but Emily saw the appreciation in the redneck's eyes for a fleeting moment before he took off down the mountainside, heading back toward Franklin.

"You think he'll make it?" Titan asked.

She stood beside him, thinking about it for a moment.

Do you think he'll make it?

She wanted to say sure, he'll be okay, but instead answered with a question of her own.

"Will any of us?"

She took a last look at the dead spider, and headed further up the mountain.

CHAPTER 18

Oral gripped the steering wheel tight as he approached Charles Street. A Facebook video was one thing, but he couldn't imagine the actual carnage that was taking place. Seeing it on a computer screen made it feel detached, like he was watching a movie. When he tried to think about it happening for real, his brain had a hard time bringing the scene to life.

That only lasted until he rounded the corner and saw firsthand the damage being done to the small town. The wheels of the SUV rolled over body parts that were stews across the road like small stumps. He jerked the vehicle to the right, smashing into one of the spiders with a reinforced bumper that sent it flying underneath the SUV only to be crushed by the weight of it.

Oral hollered in victory, bringing his hands down hard on the wheel. "Take that, you son of a bitch!"

Behind him, scores of weapons and ammunition rattled around inside duffle bags that clanked against one another. Mr. Tempo told him to bring all the firepower he could carry, and he was taking no chances. Flame throwers, grenades, sniper rifles, semi-automatics—it was a pepper's wet dream back there, minus the canned goods.

The Albright house stood halfway down the street. He kept his eyes peeled for Hazelnut, looking through the crowd of people that were gathered to defend their homes. For a bunch of civilians, they weren't doing half bad, but the spiders kept coming, and without reinforcements Oral knew it was only a matter of time before they fell, giving way to the creatures to run rampant over more streets and beyond.

He wasn't going to let that happen.

"Come on you bastards," he screamed, running down another monstrosity. This one flew over the hood and smashed against the windshield, but the SUV was more than built to handle it with multi-layer, bullet-resistant glass that could take one hell of a beating and still not shatter.

Looking in the rearview, he watched as the spider lay on the ground twitching its last breath before giving up the ghost. When his eyes returned to the road ahead, they went wide and he slammed on the breaks, bringing the vehicle to a screeching halt.

Hazelnut slapped the hood and mouthed something Oral couldn't hear. That was probably for the best. As soon as he opened the door, screams and gunfire penetrated his eardrums in a gruesome symphony that if he never heard again would be too soon.

"Hey, asshole," Hazelnut shouted. "I'm walkin' here!"

"Good to see you, too."

"Did you bring goodies?"

They ran around back and Oral opened the hatch, revealing the arsenal he'd brought with him. Hazelnut's eyes brightened.

"Thought you'd like that," he told her.

"There's more where that came from. I got the keys to a gun shop a few blocks away."

"Excellent."

"In the meantime," she said, reaching in and pulling out a flamethrower. "I say we scorch these fuckers straight back to hell."

"What'd you have in mind?"

"See how they're all spread out right now?"

Oral's gaze traveled up and down the road. She was right. There weren't more than four of the creatures grouped together. They were all hunting and killing on their own, chasing down people, climbing over houses.

"We need to find a way to get them all in one big group, preferably somewhere out in the open."

"How about a football field? I passed one a few miles back. It belongs to the high school."

"That'd work," Hazelnut agreed, "but we still need to find something that spiders are attracted to, other than us."

"Then what?"

"We drench that field in accelerant, and when they're all bunched up together, we light it up."

Oral thought about it for a moment, trying to imagine how in the world they could possibly get their hands on something that these giant spiders would be attracted to. He knew that regular spiders were attracted to insects, but he suspected there weren't enough of those around to—

A light bulb went off. A bright, shining beacon of hope that at its core seemed like insanity, but the more the idea settled in, the more sense it made that it could actually work. Besides, it was no more insane than a horde of prehistoric spiders laying waste to humanity.

"What?" Hazelnut asked, seeing the gleam in his eyes.

Oral held up a finger and tapped the comm unit in his ear. "Charlotte, this is Oral, do you copy?"

He waited a moment, and then the familiar voice of the arachnologist broke through.

Charlotte reading you loud and clear. What's up, Oral?

"Spiders like insects, right? Creepy crawlies and shit like that?"

Sure. An arachnid's main food source is insects. Cockroaches, earwigs, flies.

"What about crickets?"

Sure, crickets too. Where are you going with this?

"Conductor, are you listening?" he said, ignoring the question.

I am. What did you have in mind, soldier? Mr. Tempo responded.

"My nephew has one of those bearded dragon lizards, and the darn thing loves crickets. His mother buys them in bulk, and the label on the packaging is from some cricket farm in Georgia. I know it sounds crazy, but I need about a million of those little buggers flown here ASAP."

Say again, Oral? Did you say a million crickets?

He nodded. "Roger, Conductor. We're going to use them as bait, and then take out these sons of bitches all at once."

He watched Hazelnut's expression change from confusion to understanding as the plan hit her, and a wide smile broke out all across her face. "Fuck yeah." She nodded. "That'll work."

Let me make some calls, Oral. I'll see what I can do. Barring any hiccups, you should have your crickets in two hours. Can you hold out that long?

"Do we have a choice?" he asked.

No, Mr. Tempo said flatly.

"Then we can hold out that long. I need them dropped on the football field of Pendleton County High."

Affirmative. Good luck, Oral. Conductor over and out.

"That's genius, man," Hazelnut told him when the comm line was cut.

"We'll see. For now, we gotta get as many people on board with this as we can. We need to start gathering gasoline, cars, trucks—whatever we can use to blow these bastards to kingdom come."

Hazelnut reached into the back of the SUV and started refilling on mags, shoving everything she could into her pockets. Her stock was depleted, so Oral couldn't have shown up at a better time. "You go around and let people know," she said. "In the meantime we'll keep blasting as many of these bad boys as possible. Maybe we can move toward the high school so we can at least get them to start following us."

"I can do that. Be careful out there, Nut. Wouldn't want you to miss the bonfire."

"Just make sure you bring your marshmallows, big boy." She winked at Oral before disappearing into a crowd of people, rejoining the fray.

Oral glanced over his shoulder at another group of men who were gathered around two spiders, beating the shit out of them with baseball bats.

"Looks like the World Series starts early this year," he yelled.

CHAPTER 19

"Crickets?" Emily's eyebrows shot up as she glanced at Titan, the two of them on the same comm channel with Mr. Tempo.

Oral seems to think it might work, he told them.

"It's as good a plan as any, I suppose," Titan added.

My sentiments exactly. Where are you with finding the source of our little pest problem?

Emily peered up the mountain. "So far no sign of where these things came from. We'll keep looking, though. The Albright girl should be on her way to you now, so be on the lookout for her uncle. She needs to get to a hospital ASAP. Hopefully they'll have some sort of antivenom that can help her."

We've already got Charlotte working on that.

"Good. I'll keep you informed of our progress."

Please do.

"Cryptkeeper out."

Emily trudged on, feeling somewhat dejected that they hadn't been able to find out where these things originated, though the more she considered Oral's idea to dispose of the spiders in town, the more hope it gave her. Hope that turned to adrenaline, fueling her steps forward.

"He's a man of few words out in the field, isn't he?" she asked Titan.

"Conductor? That he is."

"How long have you known him for?"

Titan shrugged. "Long time. He was head of my unit way back when. Guy's got ice running through his veins if you ask me. One of those creatures could be staring him in the face and Conductor wouldn't even blink."

"So he used to be Delta Force?"

"Not that I know of. I used to be a Ranger, got recruited to DF on his recommendation, and the rest, as they say, is history."

Emily thought about Mr. Tempo saying he knew her father, who was a former Ranger himself. If Frank was a commanding officer, then what Titan was telling her rang true. Not that she had any reason to doubt what Tempo'd said, but it was always nice to have those nagging thoughts confirmed.

"What about you?" he asked her. "You ever serve?"

"Me? I thought about it when I was younger, but after seeing what happened to my father after his tours, it kind of soured me on the whole *be all you can be* stuff. Besides, I think I was destined for a different path anyway."

"Different? Hell, that's an understatement. How did you ever manage to get yourself involved in all this? Cryptids and shit?"

Emily laughed. Titan certainly was direct. "My grandmother," she told him. "I left home when I was seventeen and she took me in. She was an old school gypsy woman. Believed in all kinds of stuff. I sort of followed in her footsteps."

"What sort of stuff?"

"You name it. Her beliefs went beyond what you'd consider normal, even for a gypsy. Magic, spirits, weird creatures, superstitions, pretty much anything you can think of, she held it in some regard."

"No shit?"

"No shit," she echoed. "I remember one time when I was nineteen, she was telling me this story about a giant snake she'd seen when she was a little girl. She swore up and down that it swallowed a cow whole in her tiny village where she grew up, that's how big it was."

"Anaconda?"

"Maybe, but she was from Romania. I don't know of too many anacondas over there."

"So all that stuff kind of got to you, huh? Made you think there was something else out there?"

"I don't know if it made me *think* that. Really, I sort of always suspected it, but her stories and books definitely were a big influence on me. When she died, I set off on my own to research and study every weird thing I could, and here I am today, walking up a mountain in search of a giant freakin' spider."

"Crazy where life takes us, right?"

A doe darted out from behind a set of trees, startling her. Emily jumped back, clutching her chest as it heaved heavy up and down.

"Relax," Titan said.

"Sorry. After seeing what happened back in town, I'm a little on edge."

"Yeah, that was kind of crazy."

"Didn't it bother you?"

He thought about it for a moment as they kept walking. She expected him to play it cool and say it didn't get to him in the least, so she was a bit surprised by his answer.

"It scared the shit out of me."

"Really?"

He nodded. "But, as a soldier it's my job to expect the unexpected, you know? I've seen all sorts of carnage in my time. Some of it I've even caused, but it's the nature of the beast. Those things back there, I don't think of them as giant spiders, or monsters, or whatever. They're the enemy, plain and simple."

"And an enemy must be destroyed."

"Destroyed, subdued…whatever it takes to get the job done, so long as I keep people safe. You get used to those BDUs yet?"

She flinched, startled by the sudden shift in conversation, and looked down at her uniform. "It's not all bad. I'm just surprised it fit."

"Let's just say we kept in on hand for you in case."

"You mean you knew I'd be wearing this? How did you know my size?"

"Conductor. He knows everything about everybody."

"I'm beginning to realize that," she murmured, not exactly thrilled with the invasion of privacy, but it was a discussion for when she made it back.

If she made it back.

The afternoon sun beat down hard on them. It had been nearly four hours since she had arrived in Franklin. There was still at least another five hours of solid daylight left in which they had to search for some mysterious opening in the earth caused by the recent quake, and that's only if their theory was correct. For all she knew these spiders could have existed up here the entire time, and were only now becoming hostile. It was all unknown, and as used to the unknown as she was, it wouldn't hurt to have confirmation every once in a while that she was on the right track.

Lost in thought, Emily tripped over a root jutting out from the ground. She stumbled, nearly fell flat on her face, but was quickly caught by Titan, who righted her on two feet before her knees could touch soil.

"Nice reflexes," she commented.

"I may be old, but I'm not entirely useless. Maybe we should take a time out for some water."

Emily glanced around, making sure the coast was clear. The last thing she wanted to do was stop dead center of some trap. Everything looked fine, so she nodded as Titan took out a canteen and sat on a stray log off to her left.

"You've got one, too," he said, patting his chest.

She looked, and sure enough in one of the front pockets of her uniform there was a small canteen resting securely in place. The cool water sloshed down her throat, quenching her thirst. She'd been so focused on getting answers up on the mountain that she couldn't even remember the last time she'd taken a drink of anything.

"You're doing good, boss," Titan said, leaning forward and resting his elbows on his knees. "Most people I know would've lost their collective shit by now, but you're handling all this surprisingly well."

Emily felt her cheeks burn red at the compliment, and Titan smiled at her.

"Not used to those, huh?"

"No," she said. "Not really."

"I mean it," he continued. "I've been around the block—seen 'em come and go—and if I had to guess I'd say you're one of the ones that'll stick around for a while. You got some balls, and that's rare these days."

"What? For a woman to take charge?"

"No, for anybody to have balls. The world's gone soft. Too many people getting offended by Christmas cups and Facebook posts. Hell, at this rate the next world war will be started over something somebody said on Twitter. Crazy, right? All I mean is that it's nice to see someone stepping up to the plate that deserves to be there."

"Well, I don't know how long I'll be sticking around," she said honestly. "I told Tempo this was just a trial run." She took a look around at the foliage, the ground, and finally up at the bright blue sky hovering overhead. Emily took a deep breath and added, "I don't know if this is me, you know? I'm used to going it alone, being my own boss. I write books, I run a website, and occasionally get out to speak at conventions. All that's on my own dime, with nobody telling me where to go, or what to do. I'm not a leader."

She looked down at her hands, nervously picking at a thumbnail, waiting for Titan to say something. Anything. It felt good to get that off her chest, but she didn't want him to think less of her for it.

"Let me tell you something," he finally began. "Nobody's a leader. It's not something you're born with or fall into; it's something you're called to do, at the right time, in the right place. Whether you feel like you're ready or not, that doesn't matter. The world knows you're ready, and that's why you're here. To lead us through all this mess. Of course, a good leader knows when to ask for help, and you've shown that you can do that. Whether you decide to stick with it after this is entirely up to you, boss, but know that from this point forward your life is never going to be the same again, because once you've been chosen, you're going to notice opportunities hunting you down more and more until you accept your calling, and this is your calling."

Emily sat there, speechless, as Titan's words played through her head. She wanted to thank him, tell him that it was the nicest thing anybody ever told her, but instead she weathered the goosebumps on her skin, capped her canteen bottle, and stood up—feeling for the first time like a leader should, brimming with self-confidence and worth.

"Come on," she said. "Let's go finish this."

"Yes ma'am," Titan said, following right behind her.

CHAPTER 20

Mr. Tempo shoved his cell phone in his pocket and turned back to Hackman, who asked, "Did you get them?"

"One million crickets on their way."

"Isn't someone going to get suspicious as to what they're for?"

"No. It's not uncommon for reptile breeders to order crickets in bulk, and while a million of them is quite excessive, they've been told we have a lot of lizards to feed."

"How are they going to get them here?"

"Helicopter. Two Venoms are en route now from Robins Air Force Base to make the pickup. They'll be here in less than two hours to drop them on the high school football field, and hopefully by then Oral will have done what he needs to."

Hackman gave a low whistle. "Man, this is one crazy plan."

"Do you have any better ideas?"

"No."

"Then the plan isn't crazy, it's just a plan."

With that Frank Tempo made his way outside and into the tent where Michelle was still working on the giant spider carcass. He surveyed the scene, not even flinching when his arm brushed against the dead creature. Like Titan, it meant nothing to him that it was a monstrosity out of a horror movie. To Mr. Tempo it was the enemy, and he'd rather be dealing with a dead one than a live one, so any contact made with its corpse was a small price to pay.

"How's it coming?" he asked.

"Good." She held up a mason jar nearly full with spider venom. "There's two more where that came from. With any luck we won't need it, but on the offshoot that we do I've already put in some calls to Grant Memorial and they're setting up everything we'll need to make an antivenom. It'll take some time, but it's the best option we have right now."

"Excellent, and I hope you're right that we won't need it. When the Albright girl gets here I'll have her rushed to GM and we'll take it from there. Regardless, I need you to go with her and oversee things from that end."

"What about my work here?" Michelle protested. "This is the find of a lifetime, Mr. Tempo. I don't want to—"

He held up a firm hand, essentially interrupting her without saying a word. When she was quiet, Frank said, "Miss Liu, I understand your concerns, and believe me, I'm right there with you. This body will be protected, I assure you of that. When you're done with Tiffany Albright and we're sure she's safe, then we can have it transported to a secure facility where you can continue to do your work, but for now safety is the paramount concern here. We have to make sure that Grant Memorial has an antivenom in place, because there's no doubt in my mind that one little girl is not all we're going to need to treat before this is all said and done."

She placed the mason jar of venom down on the table. "You're right. I'm sorry."

"No need to apologize. This is an exquisite find for the scientific community."

"Exquisite's a good word. If this is what I think it is there's no telling the knowledge that can be learned from it. How they managed to survive for billions of years, for starters."

"Yes," Mr. Tempo nodded. "I've been wondering that myself. Do you have any theories?"

Michelle took a long, hard look at the beast before she answered, "There's any number of reasons. Slow metabolism, lack of predators, decreased air pollution underground. Still, those aren't enough to explain more than a billion years of existence. For all I know these things could've been bathing in the fountain of youth down there."

Frank snorted, stepping outside of the tent. He took off his sunglasses and rubbed the bridge of his nose. It'd been a long day, even though he'd only recently arrived in Franklin. He wanted to be there when Emily got in, but this morning he found himself meeting with representatives from the DOD, ironing out a few, last minute details for the creation of his new organization. It was so new it didn't even have a name yet, though he had a few ideas in mind to present to Emily when he saw her next.

If he saw her again.

He knew she was in good hands out there in the field with Titan at her disposal—that man was one tough soldier—but even so, this was something even he hadn't faced before, so the variables were too numerous to count when it came to making sure everyone stayed alive. Nobody knew what these creatures were capable of, though from the looks of it the only thing they seemed interested in was food. He supposed being trapped underground for billions of years really worked up an appetite.

A scream off in the distance garnered his attention, so Frank swung the rifle slung over his shoulder around, his finger staying close to the trigger guard. It had been a good long while since he'd been out in the field to even fire a weapon, but it still felt like second nature to him regardless of the passage of time. Once a soldier, always a soldier, and if one of those bastards came bursting through the trees he'd make sure it went down hard and fast.

"Come on," he whispered. "Show yourself."

Another scream, closer this time. Only it wasn't so much a scream as it was a call for help.

"Hey!" shouted the voice. "Hey! Help me."

Coming out of the trees was Sam Falkner. Sweaty, dirty, and out of breath, he lumbered forward with Tiffany in his arms, straining to hold onto her. It'd been a long trek down the mountain, and though he was a big guy, carrying a 75-pound weight all that way was taxing on the body, no matter how large you were.

"Help," he called out once more.

Frank let the rifle fall to his side, taking a few steps toward Sam. The plan was to grab Tiffany, cart her over to the waiting ambulance, and send Michelle on her way with the little girl in the hopes of treating her.

That was the plan, but as Frank knew plans rarely ever go as expected.

Crashing through the bushes, hot on Sam's heels, was a spiders. Tempo raised his gun, and Sam started to protest, stopping in his tracks and holding up Tiffany's body as if to prove he wasn't a threat.

"I got a little girl here," he screamed. "What are you doing?"

Tempo looked down the barrel of his rifle, trying to get a clear shot at the beast, but it was directly behind Sam's body, making it hard to take the shot without fear of hitting him, or the girl. His instincts were to shoot anyway, maybe the bullet would whiz by a head or shoulder and impact the creature, but it was too risky. Sam hadn't come all this way just to be shot in the face.

But he did come all this way to die.

"Get down!" Frank shouted.

Sam looked over his shoulder just in time to see the spider's fangs sink deep into his deltoids. He screamed as Tiffany's body rolled from his arms and onto the pavement, continuing to roll a few feet more. The weight of the monster on his back crippled Sam, and he crumpled to the ground, but before it could get another bite in, Frank fired into it with everything he had.

The spider shook and rattled as it was pumped full of armor piercing bullets. It hissed and gurgled, scrambling off Sam and onto the ground beside him. With each round, Frank took one step closer to it, making sure the ammo went deep, shredding it to its very core. He didn't even realize he was screaming until the firing stopped, and the creature lay dead at his feet. His chest heaved with deep, methodical breaths as Sam groaned next to him, writhing in pain. Blood poured from his wounds, and smoke from the barrel of the weapon surrounded Mr. Tempo like a fine mist.

He stood there a few moments more until the slamming of a door grabbed his attention. He whirled, saw Hackman with his jaw wide open and Michelle standing next to him at the entrance to the tent.

"Are you okay?" she called out.

Frank wasn't sure if he was okay. He felt fine, but the imprint that thing left on his mind was something that would haunt him for years to come, though he suspected that in time it would fade into the background, just like all the other moments from his past that periodically threatened to rise up from their grave.

He cleared his throat, and said, "I'm good." Then he walked over to Tiffany, ignored Sam's moans for the time being, and said, "We need to get her to safety. Take Mr. Falkner with you and see if you can tend to him as well."

Michelle ran over and scooped up the girl, rushing her to the ambulance that was being driven by men who would keep what they'd seen under wraps.

Frank threw one of Sam's limp arms over his shoulder and hoisted him up, following behind her. When the little girl was secured on a gurney and lifted into the back of the vehicle, he dropped Sam's body next to her, as Michelle took a seat next to one of the men waiting inside.

"Be well," Mr. Tempo said. Then he shut the rear doors and slapped the bumper, watching the ambulance speed away, its light and sirens as quiet as the warm country air.

CHAPTER 21

Oral topped off an empty steel oil drum with gasoline, and fastened the lid in place. Together, he and Burt Ambrose—who owned the Pump n' Save—lifted it onto the bed of Burt's pickup, placing it next to the three others they'd filled.

Burt took off his ball cap and wiped the beads of sweat from his brow. He was in his sixties, a tad overweight, but muscular. His flannel shirt was soaked through with sweat, and when he spoke Oral could see that one of his incisors was missing.

"Should we do one more?" the shopkeeper asked.

"Better to be safe than sorry, right?"

"I suspect there's a whole lot of folks who are sorry today."

Oral couldn't disagree with him.

When he'd found the man, Burt was just coming to the end of his mag. He'd screamed and thrown the empty rifle at an oncoming spider that threatened to consume him, but not before Oral could cut it down with his SCAR. After taking his hand and helping Burt to his feet, Oral asked, "Is there a gas station around here?"

As it just so happens there was, and Burt owned it, so Oral told him his plan to douse the football field, and, well, in his younger days Mr. Ambrose loved to light things on fire, so why the hell not?

Four barrels later and Burt still hadn't said much about the spiders. A bit unusual, but Oral figured he was still trying to process it all. Lord knows his brain was still trying to deal with it, and he was used to some fucked up shit.

"You say you're with the Seals?" Burt asked.

"I didn't say, but no, I'm not a Navy Seal."

"Ranger?"

"Delta Force."

Burt whistled. "Shit, I saw that movie. Chuck Norris, right?"

Oral smiled. He loved movies, and despite being historically inaccurate, Delta Force was one of his all-time favorites. "Lee Marvin, too," he said. "Did you know it was shot entirely in Israel?"

"I did not know that." Burt frowned, disappointed that such a thing could happen.

Oral stood there, the nozzle of a pump depositing gasoline into another barrel. He let the expression pass. Not everyone could be as open-minded as him.

"Mr. Ambrose?" he asked.

"Please, call me Burt."

"Okay, Burt. You don't seem to be too concerned that there's a bunch of giant spiders laying waste to your town. Is that something that happens a lot around here?"

Burt stared at him for a moment before opening his mouth, allowing the most absurd laugh Oral ever heard to escape his chest.

The big man waited for it to pass, a grin touching his lips. He couldn't help it. The laugh sounded like a cross between a mutt and a hyena having sex. "Something funny?" he asked.

"No," Burt said. "It doesn't happen around here, ever, but son, I've lived long enough to know that in these woods there's all kinds of shit no one knows about."

"What do you mean?"

"This one time I was on a hunting trip with my daddy, around ten years old. We were chasing after this buck he swore was as large as a Buick. Well, we didn't find no Buick buck that day, but we did stumble across some old caves way up high, and he got to telling me this story about a Sasquatch he'd seen when he was my age. Told me the damn thing was nearly ten feet tall, covered in black hair and looking like a gorilla."

"And you believed him?"

"Not at first, but when we got back home he showed me proof."

"What sort of proof?"

"A piece of bark from a tree, with five long scratches clawing up it. Scratches that sunk deep and hard."

Oral looked into the barrel, saw it was half full, and gazed back at Burt. "You don't think it could've been a bear?"

"Could've, but I've seen enough bear tracks in my day to know that whatever clawed that tree wasn't no bear. So, what else could it be?"

"Bigfoot," Oral answered.

"Bigfoot," Burt repeated, a wide grin plastered on his face. "So you see, a giant spider ain't nothing to me. There's all kinds of stuff in this world that ain't been discovered yet. Look at me, I just learned today that Delta Force was filmed in Israel, who's to say tomorrow I won't learn that we're just one big alien experiment?"

"Right." Oral nodded, stretching out the word as he realized that perhaps Burt Ambrose wasn't playing with a full deck. That didn't make him wrong—he was one hundred percent correct. There were things yet to be discovered. But aliens? That was a bit of a stretch, even for Oral.

He finished topping off the barrel and together they placed it next to the other four. Burt secured them in place with a bungee cord, hugging it tight around them so they wouldn't move while driving over to the high school. Then he closed the tailgate, and headed around to the driver's side.

Oral made his way back to the SUV, when Emily broke through on his comm unit.

"Cryptkeeper," he said. "Everything okay?"

We're good up here, just checking to in to see how you're doing.

"Just secured a whole bunch of gasoline. Heading over to the football field now to dump it."

And Hazelnut?

"She's back fighting the good fight. I checked in with her a little while ago. She's surviving."

That's all any of us can do right now.

"What about you and Titan? Have you figured out where these things came from yet?"

Negative, we're still searching.

Oral got behind the wheel and stared ahead, watching Burt as he tried to turn over the engine on his ancient pickup.

"Say, this is a long shot, but I'm with a guy now who said there's some caves up in these mountains."

Caves? Where?

"Hang on."

Oral hauled himself out of the vehicle again and ran over to Burt, tapping on his window.

"Might need a jump if you got cables."

"Yeah, sure," Oral told him. "Before that I need to know where those caves are."

"Caves?"

"You said you and your daddy stumbled across some caves way up high, where were they?"

Burt thought about it for a moment, recalling his own story, then said, "Near the top, I think. That was a long time ago, but I remember seeing the peak not too far off in the distance."

Oral turned away and spoke. "Cryptkeeper, those caves are somewhere near the peak."

We're not too far from there now. We'll see if we can find them. Thanks, Oral.

"Be careful, that might be where those bears we saw came from. Papa might still be around."

Copy that. Cryptkeeper out.

He turned back to survey Burt's pickup just as the older man got it running. He gave it a little gas, revving the engine. "Like a newborn kitten, isn't it?"

Oral smiled. "Sounds like it's got pneumonia."

Burt nodded toward his ear. "Who was that, the president?"

"No, just my commander. She's out—"

"She? Well I'll be damned. See, there's another thing I learned today. Come on, I'll race you to the high school."

Oral stepped out of the way before Burt could run over his foot. He made it back to his SUV just in time to see the pickup fishtail out onto the road, the barrels of gasoline shifting slightly in the back.

"Crazy fucker," he whispered.

CHAPTER 22

Hazelnut emptied her mag into a spider that tripped over the carcass of one of its buddies on the way toward her. She expelled the empty, slammed in a new one, and was on the move.

Next to her was Jim Albright, visibly relieved that they'd found his daughter, though now he was in a fight to survive if he ever hoped to see her again.

Together they headed further down the road, joined by more residents of Charles Street, and beyond, trying to draw the creatures toward the high school. It had taken a while to get the word out to people what the plan was, and even longer for them to go along with it, but after realizing that they were in a losing battle as more of them started to fall, it was the only choice they had left if they wanted to see another sunrise.

"Move, move!" Hazelnut shouted to Jim, who was slower than she was. The man was obviously aching to see his little girl again, and by God she was going to make sure that happened, even if it meant pushing him to his limits and beyond.

"Duck!" she screamed.

Mr. Albright ducked, allowing her to fire into a spider. The force of her bullets sent it flying back into someone who didn't duck, and it wasn't long before the beast was chewing its way through their torso.

"Fuck!" Hazelnut cried. Then she unloaded into it, sending it back to the hell it came from.

"We're not going to be able to do this," Jim moaned. "There's too many of them."

Hazelnut was having none of that.

As one of the only female soldiers in Delta Force, she was used to being told she wouldn't be able to do things. From the moment she signed on the dotted line in that recruitment center at the age of nineteen, her parents told her that she was making the biggest mistake of her life. She was young and smart, and if she applied herself she could be anything she wanted to be, just not a soldier. Please, not a soldier.

That was nearly fifteen years ago, and though the world's attitude had shifted over the years, Hazelnut could still feel the lingering eyes of men on her whenever she walked into a mission. Not because of her mocha skin or fit physique, but because she was a woman, and some people still couldn't handle the fact that women were just as capable as taking out the enemy as men were.

Her progression through the ranks proved it.

So to hear Jim Albright say they weren't going to make it—even though she knew he didn't necessarily mean because they were being led by a woman out in this war zone—stuck in her craw, and she grabbed hold of the man's shirt collar and hauled him just inches from her face, staring him dead in the eyes.

"You listen to me. You're going to see your daughter again, you hear? We're going to make it out of this alive, and so are the rest of these people, but you have to stay strong. If you fall apart now, you're damn right we're not going to be able to do this, so keep yourself together, man. Otherwise you'll just slow me down."

"But—"

"But nothing! You killed the spider that took your daughter. You shot it in the face and it died, up there on the mountain. Are you really gonna tell me you can't do this? Fuckin-A right you can, Mr. Albright."

She set her jaw, glaring at the man as he blinked, his eyes clearing and his spine stiffening. He nodded, and she let go of him. Hazelnut watched him straighten out his shirt, then turn around and start firing at anything with eight legs before she breathed a sigh of relief.

Close one, she thought.

She'd seen men break down before. Tougher men than Jim Albright. Men who'd been in-country with her in the early days that scoffed when she met them, only to succumb to the horrors of war and all the perils it brought with it.

Those men were long gone, and she was still standing tall, and dammit she'd be standing even taller when this was all over.

She tapped her comm unit. "Oral, this is Hazelnut, where are you?"

Just getting to the high school now. How's your progress?

"We're headed that way but it might take some time."

Do what you can. Hopefully when those crickets get here the spiders will be close enough to be attracted by them.

"They do make a hell of a racket, so here's hoping."

Copy that, Hazelnut. Stay safe out there.

"Yeah, and you try not to set yourself on fire."

No promises. Oral over and out.

She grinned and kept moving, making sure Mr. Albright was still close by.

CHAPTER 23

"Well I'll be a country fried steak," Titan said. "There it is."

Emily stood next to him, looking at the entrance to a small cave that burrowed into the mountainside. She looked up, noticing the peak wasn't too far off. "This must be the place Oral told us about. Come on, let's check it out."

"You're not worried about bears?"

She paused. "Bears? We've been attacked by giant spiders, and you're worried about bears?"

"I'm just saying." Titan shrugged. "Watch your back, that's all."

"That's your job, soldier." She winked, moving past him and into the cave.

The light seeping in through the entrance only stretched so far, and it wasn't long before they both found themselves cloaked in more darkness than she felt comfortable with. Not that Emily was afraid of the dark, it's just with those creatures running around she didn't want to accidentally stumble across one and notice before it was too late.

"Got a flashlight?"

"As a matter of fact," Titan said, yanking a small, LED tactical light free from his vest and handing it to her, "I do."

Emily clicked it on, impressed with how much of an area the beam illuminated. "You're just full of goodies, aren't you?" she said aimlessly as she wandered further into the cave.

The natural construct went deep, its walls made of stone and clay. Damp and musty, it took her a moment to get used to the odor before her senses could adjust to it. On the ground, there were large droppings consistent with that of a bear, but as far back as the light stretched, it didn't reveal any mammal waiting in the wings for them.

"Must be paying a visit to the Goldilocks' residence," Titan said, noticing the shit on the ground.

"Yeah, or looking for its wife and kids."

"How far back does it go?"

She shook her head. "I'm not sure. Far enough. Just keep that rifle ready."

"Don't have to tell me twice, boss," he said.

Emily's steps were careful and precise. The floor of the cave was slick with moisture, and one wrong move could mean a twisted ankle, or worse, a broken bone. She'd been in places like it before, in the mountains of the Sierra in Peru, searching for evidence of the mythical Machukuna, a creature of desiccated bones wandering the area in an attempt to regenerate its flesh. This cave resembled the ones she'd looked in: humid, moist, and possessing all kinds of danger that lurked in the shadows.

Yet unlike her time in Peru, where she hadn't run across anything even remotely resembling the Machukuna, something told her this mission would prove to be more fruitful. She just had to keep going.

"Look," she said, pointing ahead to an area where the cave curved to the right. "Let's see what's back there."

Titan grit his teeth together, visibly worried about what they might find.

Emily thought about telling him to buck up, but the truth was she was just as worried. Still, the thought of finally figuring out the origin of these creatures had her pulse racing. It was the closest she'd ever come to a certain discovery, something that in her line of work was rare. Sure, she'd found trace evidence and heard second-hand stories, but all that did was just offer up more questions. Now it looked like she'd finally have definitive proof of where these giant spiders had been dwelling all this time.

She just had to go a little further.

They rounded the corner, and the beam fell upon a wall of rock that signaled its end. Emily sighed, her expectations sorely disappointed by this newfound discovery.

"Son of a bitch," she whispered.

"Sorry, boss. Looks like we're going to have to keep—"

But as she moved the light around it fell upon something else. Something you normally wouldn't see in a cave. A large crack off to the right of where they'd first looked, stretching thirteen feet from floor to ceiling.

"Sweet Moses," Titan said. "Is that what I think it is?"

"Not sure yet," Emily answered, moving toward the crack, which was roughly four feet wide.

As she approached, she noticed the odor in the air switched from that of a musty scent to one earthier, as if the area beyond the crack was dry with packed dirt. She placed her hand over it to see if there was any sort of draft coming through, but there was nothing. The air was still and silent.

Dropping her fingers to the crack itself, she quickly pulled her hand away when the feeling of something wet and sticky hit her palm. She trained the light on it, revealing a mucus-like substance that was thick and gooey.

"Looks kinda like the silk from one of those spiders," Titan said, examining her hand. "Better put your gloves on."

"This could be it."

"What do you want to do?"

"I want to go in there," she told him.

"Just the two of us?"

"Everyone else is kind of busy, no?"

Titan sighed and ran a hand across his beard as his eyes fixated on hers.

Emily didn't falter. She knew he was looking for some sign of discomfort that'd tell him she wasn't entirely sure she *really* wanted to go through the crack, but she'd never been surer of anything in her life. Her mind was made up the moment they stepped foot inside the cave.

"Radio Conductor and let him know the plan. See if he can get a fix on our coordinates before we fall off the grid. I'm guessing reception in there isn't exactly high quality, so if something happens I want someone to know where to come looking for us."

"Agreed," Emily said, stepping away and tapping her comm unit. Static erupted in her ear, so she walked back around the corner until the opening of the cave came into sight, and the interference began to subside.

Tempo responded, and she proceeded to tell him what they'd found, and what she wanted to do.

Are you sure that's the best course of action? he asked.

"Right now I don't think we have a choice. Even if you just wanted us to seal it up, we still need confirmation that this is where they came from, and to do that we have to go in there."

I think it would be prudent to wait until Oral and Hazelnut have disposed of—

"We're not waiting, sir. We're going in now."

A pregnant pause filled her ear. Emily waited, unsure of how Frank would respond to her directness, though she was prepared for the worst, despite the fact he'd given her complete control of this mission.

She needed to go inside that crack to see for herself that the source of those spiders was in there. Just once. Just to gaze upon it, even if they did nothing more than turned around and waited for the cavalry to arrive.

Very well, Cryptkeeper. We've got a lock on your signal. Oral and Hazelnut will join you when they've completed their duties.

"Thank you, sir. We'll try and make radio contact, but I wouldn't count on a strong signal down there."

Noted.

Her mouth opened but nothing further came out. She wanted to apologize for being so forward, but somehow she thought that might seem weak, so she remained quiet.

Is that all, Cryptkeeper?

His voice came through flat and monotone. It was like she could hear the disappointment in it.

"Yes sir, that's all."

Then good luck, I hope you find what you're looking for.

"So do I. Cryptkeeper out."

She rounded the corner, saw Titan waiting for her as he adjusted some equipment on his BDU, and nodded. "It's a go."

"They know where we are?"

"He said they did."

They both stared into the crack, steeling their nerves. Emily's fists were clenched so tight she could feel the blood draining from her knuckles beneath the fabric of the gloves she wore.

"You su—"

"I'm sure," she said.

Feeling his eyes on her, Emily said nothing else. She put one foot in front of the other, and stepped through the crack.

CHAPTER 24

Oral stood the five drums side by side, each one containing 55 gallons of gasoline. He scratched his chin and frowned. "It's not enough."

He stared down the football field. One hundred yards. That was a lot of ground to cover, and even if they spread the drums out, tipped them on their side, and rolled them, it would maybe only take care of about two thirds of the field, if that.

"Shit," he growled.

Beside him, Buck Ambrose adjusted his ball cap—the one that said "Pump 'n Save" in big red letters—and spat a glob of chewing tobacco on the ground. "Well, this sucks," he said.

Oral rolled his eyes as the old man stated the obvious. There was no way he was going to be able to get the entire field covered in gasoline, or any other flammable liquid, before those crickets arrived. The best he could hope for was maybe setting a quarter of those spiders on fire, and what then? The others would see the danger and split, leaving them to still fight off the bastards before they destroyed any more of the town, or its residents.

It was a no-win situation.

Disappointed anger was a white-hot ball in the pit of his stomach. Oral wasn't used to failing. As a member of one of the most elite teams in the world, led by Titan, his success rate out in the field was one hundred percent. A staggering statistic when you thought about it. Somebody, somewhere, always screws up at one time or another, but not Oral.

Unless his time had finally come.

He thought about the town at his back, about Hazelnut doing her damnedest to fight off those creatures, while at the same time trying to lead them right to him because he said he had a plan.

People were counting on him for that. It was the only fucking plan they had, and now? Now it was toppling like a house of cards before his very eyes, and there was nothing he could do about it.

His brain worked overtime to try and concoct something similar, but the harder he thought about it, the more jumbled those thoughts became, mixing together in the blender of his imagination. Usually the pressure was something he thrived on, but in this case Oral felt it hard and heavy, bogging him down like a great weight placed upon his shoulders. Like the world was put on his back, and he couldn't hold it up any longer.

"Why don't you just blow it all up?" Burt said.

Oral blinked and turned to see the older man looking not at the football field but at the high school sitting right next to it. One half of the building was older, the brick weathered and fading. The other half was considerably newer, an addition in recent years. A gymnasium, by the looks of it.

"Blow what up?" he asked, his brow crinkling.

"That," Burt pointed to the school. "Few years ago they switched from electric to natural gas. You army guys always have some C4 available, right? I'm sure with those two things put together it would make a hell of a bang."

Oral scratched his cheek in disbelieving wonder. "You want to blow up the high school?"

"Why the hell not? Your idea sure as shit won't work, will it?"

Oral shook his head but said nothing. He stared at the building, thinking about all the ways it could go wrong, but he kept coming back to the one thought that mattered most: it just might work. Head down to the boiler room, cut a few gas lines to start filling it up with methane, place some bricks of C4 all around it, and boom. It was summer so there were no kids around, and the few staff that were in there could easily be cleared. There were no houses nearby, just trees and brush, so the collateral damage would be minimal.

"Son of a bitch," he whispered.

Next to him, Burt Ambrose's face broke into a wide grin. Oral looked at him, seeing for a second a hint of perverted excitement in his eyes. Like he couldn't wait to watch something burn. It sent a brief chill down his spine, but it was quickly forgotten about.

Everything was forgotten about.
The only thing that mattered was blowing up a high school.

CHAPTER 25

Psychologists refer to two ways that a mother knows when her little ones are in danger. There's the rational way, which is knowing things based on logic, and then there's the other way. The emotional way. Those feelings are based on a more primal instinct. A gut feeling, as the saying goes. That's one name for it.

Mother's intuition is another.

Deep below the surface of the earth, she knew her children were in danger. She could sense it. Feel it, almost.

Feel every gunshot wound. Feel every last breath. Feel when one of them finally died.

The nerve endings in her tingled with rage as she scurried back and forth in the cavern. Her lair. She'd given birth to her babies there. Babies that for whatever reason had never matured. Never grown. Not as big as her. That didn't make her care for them any less. She'd nurtured them. Taught them how to hunt. Taught them how to trust their instincts.

Like she trusted hers.

Something was wrong. Something was terribly, terribly wrong.

She hadn't been out of her home in a very long time. It'd become a part of her. A security blanket. Like sea turtles that never leave the ocean except to lay their eggs in the sand, she'd never left her dwelling place because it was comfortable. It was what she knew.

Now she struggled with what was comfortable, and the desire to protect her children. On the one hand she could be wrong. Maybe things were okay and she was just overreacting because they'd never been away from her for this long. On the other, on the hand she knew to be true, what if they were hurting? What if they were in desperate need of her help, and the comforts of home were nothing more than a ruse, preventing her from reaching out to them?

What if she went out there and met the same fate as them?

A great pressure built in the mother's lungs. Building and building, like the deepest of breaths being inhaled. Then, all at once, she exhaled a tremendous hiss that reverberated against the stone walls, sending rock and debris tumbling from its high ceiling.

Part of that hiss originated in frustration.

The other part was a way to build courage, much in the same way a fighter will psych himself up before a bout to get his adrenaline flowing.

This mother was a fighter.

And she was going to fight for her children.

CHAPTER 26

Mr. Tempo stood outside, hovering over the body of the spider he'd killed as Oral spoke into his ear the newly revised plan the soldier had concocted. He didn't exactly like the idea of blowing up buildings, but if it served a greater purpose then it was a small price to pay to protect the citizens of Franklin.

"At the very least it will provide us with a cover story," he said.

Exactly. Gas main explosion. Those spiders will be so torched, there'll be nothing left of them anyway.

"I'll radio the Venoms and tell them to dump their cargo on top of the school, rather than the football field." He checked his watch, then added, "ETA is seventy-five minutes, will that give you enough time?"

It'll have to, Oral said. *I'll be there shortly to grab the C4.*

"Then I'll leave it in your capable hands, soldier. See you soon. Conductor out."

He tapped his earbud, his eyes never leaving the corpse lying at his feet. Its gelatinous blood oozed onto the pavement, its eight dead eyes staring back at him while his thoughts shifted from Oral to Emily.

The determination in her voice when she'd told him that she and Titan were going into the crack wasn't what bothered him. If anything, he admired her courage.

What troubled him about that conversation was the way she'd so blatantly ignored what was clearly the better option in favor of placing her own needs above that of her safety. He knew she wanted nothing more than to find the source of these spiders, and that was fine, he did as well, but to flatly refuse waiting for backup in such a foreign situation was tantamount to committing suicide.

Who knew what they'd be walking into, let alone what they'd find. There could be a million more spiders waiting down there for her and Titan, and what then?

Maybe he'd been too quick to place her in charge of such an operation. He'd hoped that her lack of experience in these matters would prove to be beneficial rather than a hindrance. Sort of like when you hire someone new figuring they'll bring a fresh perspective to the job. Generate new ideas. The kind of ideas that escape someone with forty plus years of experience under their belt.

Now, though, he wasn't so sure he hadn't made a mistake in choosing Emily to lead his new organization.

Only time would tell, so for now he had to continue trusting she'd do the right thing, otherwise what was the point? He may as well take over. The soldiers were turning to him for guidance anyway, though he suspected that was more out of habit than because they were dismissing Emily's leadership capabilities.

When they made it through this—if they made it through it—he'd have to have a long hard look at things before deciding how to proceed.

In the meantime, he'd continue to service the mission and Emily, making sure everyone's needs were met to get the job done.

CHAPTER 27

The beam of light illuminated a trail that sloped downward at a relatively shallow angle, allowing Emily and Titan to keep their footing as they walked. She didn't know if that would change the further they went, but for now she was grateful to not have to crab-crawl down a steep incline, because she wasn't quite sure how that would work.

"Been a while," Titan said, referencing the amount of time they'd been walking for. It was hard to tell how much of it had passed, but when he looked over his shoulder the crack they'd come through was no longer visible, even when he trained his flashlight behind him. They must've been a good two miles in, if not more.

"We're on the right track," Emily told him.

"How do you know?"

She paused, and focused the tactical light on the ground. "See that stuff there?"

Titan looked to what she was pointing at, noticing a thick liquid seeping down the path off to their left, splattered in great globs that were beginning to crust over. Their color was not unlike that of cookies and cream ice cream.

"What the hell's that shit?" he asked.

"You just answered your own question."

He frowned, not understanding her meaning at first, and then the realization dawned all over his face. "You mean that's spider crap?"

Emily nodded. "Arachnids don't excrete pellet-like droppings like mice, roaches, or other pests. Theirs looks like, well, it looks like this, only on a much smaller scale."

"How do you know all that?"

"I was on this trip in Mexico one time, looking for a chupacabra. Came across some droppings I thought might belong to it, but they were from a wolf. That sent me down the rabbit hole of YouTube, and the next thing I knew I had all this knowledge about different kinds of poop. Useless knowledge, I know, but hey, I guess in this case it came in handy."

"Huh," Titan grunted. "So I guess this *is* where those things came from."

"It would seem like it."

"Do you think there's any more of them down there?"

Emily shook her head. "I don't know, but if there are we'll head back to the surface until the others arrive. I might be overzealous, but I'm not stupid."

"Conductor might have an opinion on that." Titan grinned.

"Yeah, well, he can have all the opinions he wants. I'm in charge of this mission, remember?"

"Hey." Titan held up his hands, the beam of his tactical light hitting the ceiling of the tunnel, which had stretched to a good fifteen feet above them. "You'll get no argument from me. I want to know what's down here just as badly as you do. Oral and Hazelnut work well together, so I know they're taking care of business as we speak. We've got this, Emily. Don't you worry about it, or Conductor."

"I'm not worried," she said, walking farther down the incline. "It just irks me that he'd question my judgment when he's the one who put me in this position in the first place."

"I'm sure he just wants everyone to be safe. You have to admit, just the two of us going down here all by our lonesome does seem a bit—"

"Crazy? I know. I'm used to crazy."

"That makes two of us, then," he said.

She glanced at him, saying, "I just think—"

Suddenly the ground was ripped out from underneath Emily and she began to drop. Her words turned to a shocked scream as she descended one foot, two feet, and then she was wrenched upward as Titan grabbed hold of her vest and hauled her back to solid footing.

Startled, her heart hammered in her throat as she tried to comprehend what just happened. Emily looked, shining her light to see a thirty-foot drop straight down that could've broken a leg, or worse—her neck. She breathed deep. That was almost a disaster.

"Watch your step," Titan mused, joining her in peering over the edge.

"Fuck me," she breathed hard. "That was close. Thank you."

"You're welcome. Guess we'll both have to be a little more careful from now on."

He shone his light on something that'd fallen from his own vest as he was securing Emily's weight in his grasp.

"What's that?" she asked.

"Incendiary grenade," he said.

"Great balls of fire."

"Was that a joke?"

"I don't know, was it funny?"

Titan shrugged. "Sort of."

"Come on." Emily stepped away from the drop. "Let's see if there's anything around here to help get us down there."

"Way ahead of you, boss."

She watched as Titan withdrew a ten-inch piece of metal from his pack. It was silver, slender, and looked like one of the batons they were carrying at their side.

Titan gave it a quick jolt and four metal hooks sprung out the end of it. He looped half-inch nylon rope through a hole in the handle, and said, "Step back. Just not too far back."

Emily did as he asked, more mindful of her footing this time, and Titan drew back his arm before slinging it forward with as much force as he could. The sharp hooks embedded themselves in the cave wall, the noise ringing in her ears. He tugged it hard and, satisfied, took the rest of the rope out of his pack, tossing it over the edge of the cliff.

"You're friggin' Batman, aren't you?" she asked with a twinge of humor to her voice.

"Nah," Titan said. "My parents are still alive."

"How much weight can that handle?"

"Minimum break strength is fifty-six-hundred pounds, so I'd say we're good. Come on, ladies first."

Emily took hold of the rope, carefully eased herself over the edge of the drop, and made sure her feet were secure against the rock. She'd been spelunking before, and despite the fact this was under a different set of circumstances, when she put it in that perspective it made things a whole lot easier to handle. A lot easier than imagining a giant spider waiting down below to eat her, anyway.

"I'll be right behind you," Titan said.

Emily nodded, took a deep breath, and started her descent.

CHAPTER 28

Jim Albright fired the remainder of his magazine into a spider that was gnawing on a stray cat that had the unfortunate luck to stumble across its path. He screamed, the frustration of having to fight off these monstrosities instead of being with his daughter getting the better of him, as it would any father whose little girl was in harm's way.

Beside him, Hazelnut noticed the dwindling sound of gunfire bursting all around her. People were running out of ammo, and as such more of them were falling to the arachnids. The giant creatures were learning to stick and move, becoming wise to the weapons the humans held in their grasps. As a result, more ammunition was being wasted, and less of the creatures were being put down. That meant more of them were gathering to consume their prey. Pouncing and tackling, biting and chewing, their huge jaws were filled with flesh and blood being ripped from the townsfolk of Franklin like it was mozzarella cheese fresh off a pizza.

One of them moved on Jim, but Hazelnut saw it in her peripheral, spinning and firing just as he fell on his ass in surprise. It flew out of the air and tumbled back onto someone's lawn, its legs constricting into itself as it died.

"Motherfucker!" she screamed.

"I'm sorry," Jim said. "I'm out."

She hoisted him to his feet. "It's okay. Just stick close to me."

Hazelnut looked over her shoulder to see how far they'd made it toward the high school. Off in the distance she saw it, maybe two blocks away.

She felt Jim on top of her, nudging her shoulder with his arm. He was afraid, and that was good, because she knew fear kept a person on their toes, but how many residents didn't know that? How many let it consume them and freeze up their muscles, allowing these bastards to have their way with them? Jim could stick by her all he wanted to, but there were still hundreds more people that couldn't. People that were out in the street, their weapons now useless—good for nothing more than being used as a bludgeoning tool that had very little effect unless used in a group.

"Behind you!" Jim yelled.

She spun, fired, and screamed.

Firing and screaming. Firing and screaming.

All while hoping that Oral was busy fulfilling his half of the bargain they'd made to take down the spiders all at once. The plan was a long shot, she knew that, but it was all they had. There weren't enough guns or ammo to go around, and even if she made her way to the gun shop that Sam owned, it looked like there'd be considerably less people to take up arms against the enemy than there were those eight-legged sons of bitches running rampant. She'd tried to do a count when this began, but lost her way when she hit a hundred and twenty-three.

Yet she moved on, with Jim at her side, and those remaining fighting the good fight.

Firing and screaming.

Firing and screaming.

It was all she could do.

It was all any of them could do at this point.

CHAPTER 29

The SUV came to a screeching halt, the engine still running as Oral jumped out from behind the wheel. He saw the tent where Michelle had been doing her work, then he looked and saw the dead spider Mr. Tempo killed before sending her on her way with Sam and Tiffany in the ambulance. Frank stood next to the carcass, looking out of sorts in his black suit, a rifle still slung over his shoulder.

"Jesus," Oral said. "What the hell happened here?"

Mr. Tempo turned toward him. "Pest control," he said flatly.

"Yeah, I guess there's a lot of that going around, huh?"

Tempo nodded. "The C4 is in a duffle bag on the Bus waiting for you. Detonator's on the shelf."

"Copy that."

Oral hauled ass inside command central, heading down the wide aisle and past Hackman, who sat at his computers monitoring everything from afar. He patted the young technician on the shoulder as he went by, drawing John's attention.

"How's it going out there?"

Oral bent, unzipped the duffle bag, checked to make sure everything was in place, then grabbed the detonator he'd use to blow everything to kingdom come.

"It's the fucking apocalypse, man."

Hackman swallowed, his prominent Adam's apple bobbing.

The two men met each other's gaze. Oral looked hard into his eyes, waiting for Hackman to glance away. To flinch. After all, he was just a kid. Spent his days playing on computers. He couldn't possibly understand what it was like out there right now, no matter how many videos he watched, or how many Facebook profiles he sequestered.

But Hackman didn't flinch, and for a fleeting moment there passed a mutual respect between them. The kind of respect that can only come from being in the same trench together, despite being from two different worlds. They didn't have to like one another. Hell, Oral still wasn't sure he wouldn't walk right by the kid if he was being mauled by one of those creatures out there, but for one second—one moment—they were brother's in arms.

Even if Hackmans arms were the size of grade school pipe cleaners.

Oral shouldered the bag and took a few long strides before reaching the front of the Bus.

"Hey," Collett called after him.

Oral glanced at him, still keeping his shoulders square.

"Sorry about the whole Pornhub thing," he said.

The soldier considered his apology, nodded, and replied, "I prefer Brazzers. Sign me up for that, and we're good."

Hackman's thin lips spread into a wide grin. "You got it."

"Be safe in here," Oral said, looking around the confines of the Bus.

"You be safe out there. When you get back I'll show you some hot MILF action, deal?"

"Kid, you read my mind."

Oral stepped into the fresh air, noticing Mr. Tempo still lingering over the spider's dead body. He put the duffle bag of C4 in the SUV, and went over to the man who'd brought them all together. Even though Frank was shorter than he was, when Oral stood next to him he could feel Tempo's intimidating presence radiating in circles around him. It didn't necessarily make him nervous, just cautious, the way you should be when dealing with someone in a position of great power.

"Shouldn't be long now," Mr. Tempo told him.

Oral wasn't sure if he meant the arrival of the crickets or their imminent doom that seemed to be lingering on the horizon if this plan went south. There was no backup. This was their one chance, and if it somehow got fucked up...

He didn't want to think about that. It would work. It had to. It was mostly Hazelnut's idea, but when the two of them put their heads together things usually turned out for the best.

This wasn't going to be the exception to the rule.

He stuck out his hand. Mr. Tempo looked at it, then up at Oral, who stood with his jaw set and his eyes burning with determination. When Frank took it, the big man said, "We won't let you down, sir."

"Good hunting, soldier."

He released his grasp, and darted for the SUV filled with explosives.

CHAPTER 30

Emily and Titan stepped through a wide opening leading into a massive cavern that spread out before them like the mouth of a great beast.

She craned her neck, looking all around as a sense of complete wonder filled her from head to toe like never before. She'd explored the Amazon, been to the Ellsworth Mountains in Antarctica, and while those places held a special place in heart, they'd been traversed before. This was fresh ground, never before touched by the foot of man until now. It was every explorer's dream to discover something new, and this day brought with it not one but two new discoveries that she'd cherish until the day she died.

Which wasn't going to be today. Not if she had anything to say about it.

"Pretty amazing, isn't it?" she asked Titan, glancing over at him.

He'd stopped beside her, his jaw hanging somewhat slack while he took it all in. Yes, he was a soldier, but she could see it in his eyes that he was just as enthralled with this newfound discovery as she was. He had a bit of explorer in him as well. He'd have to for him to be so intrigued by their surroundings.

"When I was a kid," he said, "they were building a shopping mall near our house. My friends and me used to go in there and play when it was still under construction. The foundation, all those steel beams yet to be covered up. Hell, it didn't even have a roof yet. It was like playing inside the skeleton of a dragon. This reminds me of that."

Emily turned her attention to the walls and ceiling, the beams from their tactical lights illuminating rock and clay and stalactites hanging high above them. Up the side and overhead there was what looked to be some sort of plant life clinging to the cavern. Hundreds, perhaps even thousands, of little protrusions that resembled garlic bulbs clustered together in bunches spread out over seemingly random intervals. Some were an off-white color, while others had twinges of soft blues and green to them.

She switched off her flashlight, directing Titan to do the same. "Humor me," she said.

He hesitated, but did as she asked, and all at once the bright light around them switched to dull hues of dim colors that washed over the cavern, reminding Emily of being a darkroom developing photographs.

"What the hell?" Titan marveled.

"They're bioluminescent," she said. "Chances are they're some sort of fungus."

"I ain't never heard of no glow-in-the-dark mold before."

"It mostly happens in marine life, but it's been recorded in some above-ground fungi, as well as bacteria over the years."

"Bacteria?" Titan questioned, his brow rising with caution.

"Don't worry, it won't make you sick. At least, I don't think it will."

"Well, doesn't that just set my mind at ease."

Emily stepped further into the cavern, the way lighted for her enough to tell that there were no drop-off's she had to be on the lookout for. Her feet were on solid yet somewhat slick ground, the soles of her boots gripping with each step, preventing her from slipping.

"Look," she said, pointing forward.

Across the way, perhaps a quarter of a mile ahead of her, there was another opening, smaller than the one they'd come through, though still impressive. Emily tried to adjust her eyes to peer into it, but the soft lighting from the fungus all around them wasn't enough to bring to light the darkness that spread down the chamber.

"What do you want to do?" Titan asked.

The wonder she'd been experiencing was replaced with purpose, the gravity of their mission returning front and center to her mind. As much as she'd like to hang around and gawk at their current surroundings, they still had a job to do, and as best as she could guess their way led into the darkness beckoning her forward.

The excitement of what else they may find jolted her, and Emily switched on her flashlight. Titan did the same, and together they made their way across the cavern, two ants dwarfed by its immense size.

Halfway across the great divide between one opening and the next, she paused, training her hearing on the walls and ceiling. Cocking her head, she tried to zero in on it, holding her lungs so that her own steady breathing wouldn't get in the way.

"What is it?" Titan whispered.

Emily held up a hand, signaling for him to be quiet. When he stopped moving, and they were both standing statue still holding their breath, she heard it. A low, methodical drumming. A hammering, almost, coming from beyond. Somewhere far, yet as she continued to tune in, it became apparent that wherever—or whatever—it came from was coming closer.

"I don't like the sound of that," Titan murmured, his lips barely moving.

Emily didn't, either. Goosebumps spread out all over her clammy flesh. It was already nearly twenty degrees cooler down here than on the surface, and the chill that tingled its way down her spine sent an ice cold shiver through her, heightening her senses, as well as the adrenaline coursing through veins that felt just as guarded as she did.

The hammering grew in her ears, sounding not like the beat of one drum, but the beat of many. Three, four, maybe five drums beating louder and louder.

No, not five.

Eight.

Eight drums.

Eight, heavy drums that weren't drums at all.

They were legs.

The realization dawned on Titan at the same time, and they looked at one another. The air around them became charged with fear. Joining those eight, pounding legs was a hiss that echoed through the chambers opening and bounced off the walls and ceiling before reverberating back to them, causing her goose pimpled flesh to begin trembling.

"Remember when I said if we found any more spiders we'd head back to the surface and wait for backup?"

"Yeah," Titan said.

"I think now would be a good time to do that."

But before either of them had a chance to tuck tail and run, they were met with the source of the hammering as it burst forth from the chamber.

It wasn't any more *spiders*.

It was one. Singular.

One spider.

Bigger than any bathtub she'd ever seen.

"Get behind me!" Titan yelled.

Before she knew what was happening he shoved her with a thick arm, shielding her body with his own before gunfire erupted all around them.

CHAPTER 31

1st Lieutenant Greg Baldwin moved the cyclic stick forward, pitching the nose of the UH-1Y Venom downward, dropping altitude as Pendleton High came into view. Beside him, 2nd Lieutenant Calvin Frost looked over his shoulder at their cargo: 50 boxes, each containing 10,000 crickets.

Another Venom was behind them, carrying the same.

"What do you think they're for?" he asked.

Baldwin shook his head. "Who the hell knows? I just wanna drop 'em and get outta here before we run outta fuel."

"Think we'll make it to Langley?"

"We're pushing it, but it's all good. Bird'll be in the nest, and we'll be back in our bunks before sundown."

Frost stared at the crickets. Even through the *thwock thwock thwock* of the rotor blades muffled by his headset, he could hear the bugs chirping. It gave him the willies. One or two crickets weren't too bad. Five was even no big deal.

500,000 of them though, all bunched together like that? Shit, it made his skin crawl.

"What the—"

Frost turned around and saw what Baldwin was looking at. Beyond the high school, smoke billowed up into the air. It was hard to tell where it was coming from, but from the looks of it a fire had started near a residential area that threatened to spread to nearby houses.

"What do you make of it?" the 2nd Lieutenant asked.

Bright bursts of light peppered the area beyond the flames, like those emanating from a rifle. "Looks like a friggin' war zone down there," he answered.

He saw tiny shapes scurrying about, but it was impossible to make out what they were without losing focus on the task at hand. As much as he'd like to investigate, they were given an order—a job to do—and the primary goal right now was dumping their load.

"Get ready," he told Frost, maneuvering the Venom closer to the school.

The soldier unbuckled his harness and went into the cabin, securing himself beside the 50 boxes. There were five rows, each stacked ten high. On the side of each box there was a stamp that read Georgia Crickets.

Frost took a utility knife from his pocket, grabbed one of the boxes, and sliced through the packing tape holding it closed. He opened the flaps, and cringed when he saw thousands of crickets crawling over pieces of egg crate that had been placed inside, allowing them to maneuver around instead of crawling all over the bottom.

"Little bastards," he said. "It's time to go for a ride."

Then he picked up another box, and did the same.

CHAPTER 32

Oral placed the last of the C4 bricks on the main doors to the high school, and hauled ass out of the building.

He ran towards Burt, who was displaying a smile with teeth that were stained brown from all the tobacco he chewed day in and day out. The older man had done his part, going down into the boiler room while Oral was at the Bus grabbing the explosives, releasing the valves from the pipes that pumped natural gas through the building, allowing methane to snake its way through the corridors. It hadn't been filling for very long, but Oral knew once those C4 bricks were detonated, the lingering gas would be enough to send the entire building sky high.

It would be an explosion to rival that of any fireworks display, that much was for damn sure.

"Come on." He grabbed Burt by the arm. "We gotta get clear."

"Think it'll be enough?"

Oral chanced a look over his shoulder. "We got twenty blocks in that place. If those spiders survive that, I'll eat *your* hat."

Burt secured his ball cap in place with a weathered hand. "The hell you will," he said.

"Don't worry," Oral continued, jogging further away from the building, "I won't have to."

At least he hoped he wouldn't. He didn't know much about these prehistoric spiders, but he knew enough about explosives to know whether you were ten years or ten billion years old, when the nitrogen and carbon oxides released and expanded at a rate of 26,550 feet per second, shit was going to get messy.

Heads would roll, as the saying went.

He just didn't want it to be his head.

So he ran, and Burt ran, and when they were far enough away they both turned around and did the only thing left to do.

They waited.

CHAPTER 33

The spider was unlike anything her imagination could have concocted. Emily wasn't even sure she would call it a spider. It was the size of a Humvee with eight legs jutting out of it. Three on each side toward the rear, and two near the front used for grappling.

The body was a mass of what looked to be stone and clay, like it had been down here for so long that the very caves it dwelled in had become a part of it. Molded and conformed to it over the course of billions of years to the point where it was hard to distinguish between the two. It was as if the very cavern itself had come alive.

Unlike the smaller ones back in town that were covered in fine hairs, this creature was just a triangular block with eight eyes and two, very large and very scary fangs that stretched more than half Titan's body length.

And Titan was a big fucking guy.

Emily held her ground behind him as he fired at the beast, doing his best to keep it at bay. Chucks of stone chipped free from the creature, but it didn't seem like any significant damage was being done to it. She'd joined in the fray, firing her own rifle and nearly falling on her ass in the process, but he'd told her to stop. To conserve their ammunition as best they could because they'd need it to get out of here.

They both fell back at a slow pace, making their way through the cavern toward the entrance they'd come through. She had no idea what they were going to do once they reached the thirty-foot drop she'd nearly tumbled down. It was going to be hard to hold off this thing and try to climb at the same time.

She tried to radio the Bus, but her ear was filled with nothing but static, just like she suspected it would be.

Over the noise of rapid gunfire, she could still hear it hissing. A crazed, frantic sound threatening to drive her mad with fear and anxiety while the creature continued to advance on them.

Coupled with that was Titan's screams. She couldn't imagine what he was feeling. He was used to firing on the enemy and that being the end of it. In this case it didn't look like he was anywhere near finished with this thing. It kept coming, and coming, and coming. No matter how many rounds of ammo he fired into it, it crawled and hissed, its two front legs trying to ward of bullets as it moved.

"Goddammit," she yelled. "We need backup."

"Oh, *now* we need backup," he shouted back. "Thank you, captain fucking obvious."

Emily winced. That was fair. She deserved everything he had to throw at her. After all, she was the one who got them into this mess, and while her heart hammered in her ears, she looked all around for a way to get them out of it, but her mind drew a blank.

They were going to die down here.

She just hoped it would be quick.

CHAPTER 34

Hazelnut dug her heels into the dirt and held her ground. Behind her, a block away, she could see Pendleton High standing tall, while in front of her the remaining townsfolk with weapons stood steadfast in their desire to rid their town of these pests.

The residents whose weapons ran dry had either fallen to the spiders or taken shelter indoors in the hopes of surviving. Some were lucky and managed to barricade themselves behind solid walls, while others weren't as fortunate. She'd watched one woman in cutoff shorts and a tank top get mauled by one of the beasts. It'd taken hold of her long blonde hair, pulling her back with such force her neck snapped before she hit the ground. From there her body was easy pickings for the creature, and it'd sunk its fangs into her breasts, piercing straight through her ribcage.

Jim Albright stood next to her, firing a SIG she'd handed over. Shell casings littered the ground around them.

"This is it," she said. "This is as far as we go."

"Now what?" Jim asked.

"Now we wait."

She tapped her earbud, making contact with Oral.

"Oral this is Hazelnut, what's your twenty?"

No answer.

"Oral, I repeat, this is Hazelnut. What's your position?"

She waited, and was met with silence on the other end of her comm unit. Hazelnut felt her stomach drop as it filled with worrying pangs that threatened to consume her. Oral couldn't have fallen. Not now. They were almost there. Almost to the point where they'd see their plan through to fruition. If he was dead, it meant there'd be no one at the school to light it up, and thus once those creatures got done feasting on crickets, they'd turn their attention back to the town.

"Shi—"

Hazelnut this is Oral, come in.

"Oral, you son of a bitch, where you been?"

Don't talk about my momma like that. I was waiting to get secure. We're on the other side of the school.

"Everything set?"

Bet your ass it is.

Hazelnut's pulse quickened. This was it. Their last stand. She felt newfound electricity shoot through her blood, awakening her senses, her courage, her pride…everything. This was their moment to shine.

But while she looked around at more and more townsfolk continuing to fall victim to the spiders, it was hard for her to latch on to any of those feelings, because her and her team had failed to protect those that were now lying dismembered in the streets. *Such is war*, she told herself, but war wasn't supposed to happen at home. Where you laid your head down at night and dreamed of good things. Pure things.

This wasn't war.

It was a nightmare brought to life.

Yet there was still hope that it could all be brought to an end, and as long as she still had life in her, Hazelnut would make sure that she saved as many people as she could.

She took a few steps forward, screamed, and fired, blasting one spider, and another, and another.

And in the distance, the sound of two UH-1Y Venom copters incoming made her pull the trigger that much harder. Scream that much louder.

It was done.

They were almost done.

CHAPTER 35

Oral shielded his eyes as the two Venoms made their way overhead. Their cabin doors were spread open, and he could see a man in each. Beyond them, boxes of crickets were at the ready to be dropped.

"There they are," Burt marveled. "Shit, look at those things. They kinda look like Hueys."

"You know your birds," Oral said. "Those are the UH-1Ys, they replaced the 1Ns a little while ago."

"God bless America," Burt said.

"Amen to that."

Amen to all of it, he thought. They were finally going to get to go home and be done with this mess. It'd been a long fucking day, and Oral wanted nothing more than a hot shower and a cold bottle of beer. He wanted it so bad he could taste the hops on his tongue.

Burt spat a glob of tobacco gunk beside him. Oral glanced at it, and said, "Don't you know that shit'll kill you?"

"Please," the old man said. "When you're my age a piece of bacon can kill you."

"Or a spider," Oral joked.

They stared at one another for a moment, then both men broke into a fit of laughter, releasing all the tension that'd built up over the last couple of hours. They'd been going hard and fast, never stopping to breathe, and the helicopters now hovering above the high school were a sight for their sore and tired eyes.

It was almost done.

Oral stood from a crouched position as the first box of crickets began to fall. He pumped his fist into the air, yelling, "Bombs away, motherfuckers!"

Then he waited for the spiders to show up.

CHAPTER 36

The spiders didn't notice the crickets. Not at first, anyway. They continued on their path of destruction, rampaging through town and grabbing anything that moved. They'd never had a feast like this. Ever. It was sensory overload for them. A meal fit for a king, or an army.

Jaws crushed bone and ripped flesh, while fangs became stained with the blood of men and women who, just that morning, had never envisioned their death to come at the hands of a creature so horrendous. So merciless. The spiders ate and ate and ate, and when they were full they hunted for the sheer thrill of chasing something down for the first time in their lives. Everything they'd consumed up until this point had been caught in a web. An unsuspecting mole traveling too far down. A groundhog that'd trapped itself in the sticky substance, only to lie there waiting to die.

It was fun, it was exercise, it was everything a spider could want.

And now there was more.

One noticed the chirping first, then another, and another.

Slowly the noise began to build, tickling the prickly hair all over their bodies. It wasn't like the screams they'd become used to hearing, or the *tat tat tat tat* that came from those things the humans held in their hands. The things that hurt them. This was a new noise. One on an entirely different level that was impossible to resist.

One by one, they gravitated toward it. Some crawled cautiously over fences and houses, while others moved quickly, eager to be the first to explore such a discovery. What could make such a beautiful symphony of sound like that? What wonders awaited them upon their arrival?

They left intestines in their wake, body parts strewn across grass and concrete, and rivers of blood flowing into storm drains. Some fell when they turned their backs on the humans, allowing their bullets to penetrate and kill. Most made it safely away, weaving through the trees and brush that led up to the high school, as the wind picked up all around and blew the scent of something sweet and delicious their way.

It was going to be glorious.

CHAPTER 37

"Not today, you eight-eyed son of a bitch!" Titan shouted. He dropped his magazine, quickly grabbed another, and punched it home. It was the second to last one he had on him, though he knew Emily had more. He chanced a look back over his shoulder, his finger on autopilot as the rifle shot round after round at the monstrosity. "Shit," he growled.

They'd barely made it back to the wide mouth of the cavern they'd found themselves in. Emily was close by, doing her best to provide moral support, but through her tough exterior he could see the fear in her eyes. The worry. He felt somewhat guilty for snapping at her, but it wasn't enough to completely quench the disdain he had roiling in the pit of his stomach.

Not for her, but for himself.

He knew better than to proceed on a mission like this without backup, and he should've said something at the time rather than follow her blind into that fucking crack. Look where it'd gotten them. Smack dab in the middle of some freaky shit, and now he didn't know if they were going to make it out alive. He'd been in some hairy situations in his day—Fallujah, Kandahar, Syria—but even the tumultuous Middle East couldn't compare to the horror he was facing here, at home.

Whipping his head around, he took a step back. The spider took a step forward. It was only a matter of time. He'd run out of ammo sooner rather than later, then he'd run through whatever Emily had on her, and then…what? Would the spider kill them right away? Save them for later? Fuck, he didn't want to think about it.

Hell, if it came down to it there was a good chance he'd put a bullet in his head, but not before Emily suffered the same fate.

God, all those tours, all those missions, only to be done in by a goddamn spider. What were the odds?

Another glance at the woman who was supposed to be leading them all saw Titan do a double take. No longer was she looking at the spider, but instead her focus was on the ceiling above them. She caught him looking at her, and pointed up rather than try and yell over the hissing and shooting and screaming.

Titan looked, seeing the stalactites hanging above them. He'd forgotten they were there. He'd been too busy trying to put down the beast with raw power that the thought of using anything else never occurred to him. Now? It was worth a shot.

He nodded, still keeping his weapon trained on the spider. Behind him, he heard Emily's rifle start to go off, sprinkling them in rock and dust and debris that descended from the ceiling. It was a virtual hailstorm, and over the noise of everything the tearing away of rock sounded like a crack of thunder rolling through him. One of the stalactites come crashing down onto the cavern floor a few feet away from the spider.

The beast jumped back, surprised by this new threat.

Titan grinned, and shouted, "Keep going!"

Emily didn't falter. He kept listening as her rifle discharged again and again. From the sound of it she was trying to take aim, something he wouldn't even bother with. He'd just point and shoot, hoping for the best, but not her.

Of all the things to be meticulous about, she chooses that, he thought. *Fuck me.*

But it was working. More and more of the great mineral formations began to fall. The spider was trying to dodge them, but they were nipping at its heels, taking chunks of rock off it that sent it scrambling backwards in surprise, and—hopefully—pain.

When it looked like he might be able to take a breath, Titan aimed the barrel of his rifle at the ceiling and together with Emily he began firing. The sound of thunder intensified, the entire cavern vibrating around them. For a second it reminded him of his time in Malaysia and this one hotel he'd spent a long night in. The bed was equipped with a machine that, when fed a quarter, shimmied and shook in what was supposed to be some sort of therapeutic massage, but it rattled the back of his teeth so much he ended up sleeping on a hard-backed lounge chair. The vibrations he felt now were like that, only this time it wasn't just the back of his teeth rattling, it was his entire fucking head.

Then all at once the ceiling began to fall, and together they lowered their weapons and started running. Titan's legs moved in long strides, but Emily was considerably shorter than he was, and it wasn't long before he was passing her. On the way by, he placed a hulking arm around her back and lifted her five inches off the ground, sprinting toward the mouth of the cavern.

Almost there, he thought. *Almost there.*

CHAPTER 38

Calvin Frost dumped box after box of crickets over the side of the Venom as it hovered over the high school. At first he'd tried to dump them out of their containers, but the wind from the rotor blades above him blew the insects every which way but down. The boxes didn't fair much better, but at least the majority of them were landing on the building, not on the ground beside it.

Twenty down, thirty to go.

He'd tried to fathom the purpose of all of this. He and Baldwin were tasked with this order, which seemingly came out of nowhere. One minute they were on a training exercise, and the next they were being asked to pick up a metric shit ton of crickets from some farm in Georgia. It seemed odd that any branch of the military would be ordered to do such a pedestrian job. Wasn't this what FedEx was for?

He shook his head, watching the little suckers fall while the pilot held the bird steady. Maybe it was some kind of science project for the kids. After all, what else could one million crickets be used—

Frost stopped, a box clutched in his hands ready to go. He wasn't sure what he was seeing, but it looked to be…were those…spiders? Coming closer? What the hell?

He yelled into his headset, "Are you seeing this?"

Baldwin responded with a shaky affirmative, and Calvin blinked, thinking that maybe his eyes were playing tricks on him. No, that didn't sound right. If the pilot were seeing them too, that wouldn't make sense. How could both of their eyes be playing the same trick?

"God," he whispered. "What the hell are those things?"

But he knew. He didn't want to know, but Lord help him, he knew. Giant spiders, hundreds of them, crawling all over the school as the crickets hopped around, trying to escape their huge jaws.

He dropped the box, grabbed another, and picked up the pace.

A movie. That's what they were for. Some sort of horror movie they were filming. Those things couldn't be real. They were too big, too grotesque. Only a special effects guy could create something like that.

But a little bird in the back of his head told him that wasn't right, either. That's what CGI was for. No way a movie would use so many practical effects like that. It would cost too much money.

So what options did that leave?

Another box fell, and another, and another. His hands were shaking by this point, and the saliva drained from his mouth leaving his tongue to feel like rough sandpaper.

At least the Venom was high enough to avoid the creatures. It was nearly a hundred feet above the high school. No way a spider could jump that high. Not even those tiny jumping spiders he'd seen on TV. Those buggers were cute, though. Not like these things. These were…Frost didn't even have a word for what these were. Ugly didn't seem to do them justice. Ugly was just a—

One of the spiders jumped, snatching a falling box from mid-air.

"Shit," Frost shouted, more out of surprise than anything. "Take us up," he yelled. "Take us up."

But Baldwin hadn't seen the spider jump.

"I can't. We go any higher and we'll waste 'em," he answered, referring to the crickets. He knew as well as Frost did that their mission was to dump them *on* the high school. Not beside it.

Another spider jumped. A little higher this time. Calvin looked at it. He could swear all eight of its black, soulless eyes were trained on him. "Take us up," he yelled again, this time panic filling his voice. "They're gonna get us!"

"They're not gonna—" Baldwin started to say.

Then a third spider leaped into the air, grabbing hold of the Venom's landing skids with two of its legs. The helicopter lurched down and to the side, the remainder of the cricket boxes tumbling out. Frost latched onto of the door, one foot faltering before he could get grounded.

"Jesus!" he screamed.

The six remaining legs on the spider moved about in a frenzied mess of twirls and grabs until another leg found purchase. Then another. The two remaining free dangled beneath the creature, and Calvin heard the bastard hiss just as another one jumped on to its back and scrambled up the length of it, getting close enough to take hold of the 1st Lieutenant and haul him overboard.

The last thing Calvin Frost saw before dying were the fangs of nine spiders all grouped together, waiting to rip him apart.

CHAPTER 39

"Holy shit," Oral said, quickly tapping his earbud and continuing, "Oral to Conductor, do you copy?"

Conductor here.

"We've got spiders on the bird. Repeat, spiders on the bird."

There was a brief pause before Mr. Tempo asked, *Is the bird down?*

"One of its babies is. Flew right into a gang of spiders. It's not looking good."

And the other?

"Other bird just cleared the nest, all cargo dispatched."

Blow it, Tempo told him.

"Repeat for clarification," Oral asked.

I said blow the damn building, soldier.

"Roger that, Oral out."

He glanced at Burt, who was looking at the scene with wide-eyed wonder as the helicopter was overrun with giant beasts. The rotator blades, spinning at a rate of 675 feet per second, sliced and diced some of them to bits, sending legs and bodies soaring, while others were crawling over one another to get inside the cabin. The Venom lurched once more, coming that much closer to crashing.

"What'd he say?" Burt asked.

"He wants me to blow it," Oral whispered, looking at the carnage taking place.

He felt bad for the young soldiers. For the one who'd already died, and for the one that was about to. Though he imagined a quick death from the explosion would be better than being ripped to pieces by those bastards. God, they had no idea what they were getting themselves into, and now someone would be notifying their families of their death, probably with the training exercise excuse.

If people knew how many of their loved ones died in something that most definitely was not a training exercise, there'd be outrage.

Beads of cold sweat broke out all over Oral's upper lip. He licked it away, and took hold of the detonator at his side that would remotely send a signal to the bricks of C4, shocking them full of heat waves that would initiate the explosion.

All he had to do was press a button.

A part of him hoped that the bird would still fly. That maybe the pilot would be able to regain control enough to soar away, high and wide, while the spiders gave up the hunt and dropped to the ground. But as much as he hoped that would happen, as the seconds ticked by the Venom continued to fall, losing altitude.

"Go on, what are you waiting for?" Burt coaxed. "Blow it!"

Oral whispered, "Yeah," said a quick Our Father, and pressed his thumb down hard on the detonator.

All at once the high school blew into a great ball of fire, the explosion burning hot and high. Chunks of brick, plaster, steel, and spider, landed everywhere. Oral and Burt were safe enough away to not have to worry about debris, but they felt the shockwave from the blast as it blew the old man's ball cap right off his head.

"Whooohoooo," Burt shouted.

Oral hung his head, smelling the explosion. It burned at his nose hairs, but it was over.

Almost.

The sound not unlike that of a jet engine preparing for takeoff momentarily filled the air around them, and then a second blast even bigger than the first lit up the dusky evening sky like the sun had risen before its time.

Natural gas, Oral thought.

A huge fireball rolled into the air, burning orange and black. The high school, the spiders, and two hundred yards of surrounding grass and trees were consumed in the white-hot blast that rumbled the earth beneath their feet, leaving behind nothing but a deep crater that Oral suspected could probably be seen from space.

The rumbling continued.
The ground began to shake.
But the spiders were dead.
All of them, except for one.

CHAPTER 40

Mr. Tempo stood with one foot resting on a bench just outside the Bus. In the distance he saw the fireball light up the sky, took off his sunglasses, and allowed his naked eyes to gaze upon the orange and back smoke as it licked the air.

His job wasn't easy. It never had been, and he suspected that it never would be. Making the tough calls was something he'd done throughout the years, each one more taxing than the last. They haunted him on occasion, when he awoke in the middle of the night covered in sweat with the bed sheets tangled around him. The ghosts of those tough calls lingering over his paralyzed body, asking *what if?*

What if you waited?

What if you held on just a little longer?

What if?

Tonight, two young servicemen would join them.

He never wanted anybody to die, but his mentality was that of serving the greater good. If he hadn't told Oral to blow the building when he did, who knows what would've happened. He could be overrun by spiders right now. Him, Hackman, the Bus. Everyone.

He wondered if Emily would've been able to make that call.

He wondered if Emily and Titan were still alive, or if they'd be joining the chorus of *what ifs* along with those two servicemen.

As Frank lowered his raised foot to the ground, he felt a rumble beneath him. He stiffened, hoping it would pass, but it didn't. It was like the ground was coming alive, and a few seconds later Hackman came bursting out the door to the Bus.

"Sir, we have a problem. The USGS is reporting—"

"Seismic activity. Yes, I know."

Hackman looked at him, a question on his face.

Mr. Tempo knew a lot of things, and right now he knew they had to get the hell out of there.

He dashed into the tent, took hold of the dead spider Charlotte had been examining, and with all his strength he pulled it inside.

CHAPTER 41

Emily spun just as they cleared the threshold out of the cavern. The spider was buried under a mountain of rock and mineral, the weight of those stalactites all but crushing it. Her chest heaved, her muscles were on fire, and the ringing in her ears was constant, but she was alive. Titan was alive.

They'd made it.

"Jesus Christ," Titan said, leaning over to catch his breath. "That's one tough son of a bitch. I ain't never seen a spider like that, have you?"

Emily didn't bother justifying his question with an answer. She simply glared at him and the lopsided grin on his dusty face. She thought he'd still be pissed at her for leading them almost to their deaths, but the big man stood and patted her shoulder. He was in much better spirits now that the threat had passed.

"We need to get out of here," she said.

"I hear that. I need a shower and a beer."

Emily nodded, looking at the massive pile of rubble in the middle of the cavern as loose rocks and debris tumbled off it. Titan did the same, and together they stared in silence as if making sure that what was dead would stay buried.

She didn't think they'd make it. In the heat of it all, she thought for sure that her death would come at the hands of a creature she'd hunted for her whole life. Maybe not this particular creature, but what it represented was a lifetime of searching. Now, she had answers. As many as she needed to keep pressing forward, because even if no one ever found about what once dwelled beneath the mountains of West Virginia, she knew, and for now that was enough.

"Come on," she bumped Titan's forearm. "Let's get you that beer."

They turned, and that's when she felt it.

The ground started to shake and shimmy, nearly knocking both of them off their feet. Emily clutched the tunnel's wall for support, feeling the vibrations rumble through her, as if on the other side of it a subway train was burrowing past them.

But this was no train.

She looked to Titan for confirmation and saw the fear in his eyes.

"Earthquake," he shouted. "We got to fucking move, now!"

A garbled hiss came from behind them and she looked back to see the giant spider emerging from its tomb. Large rocks fell from the top of it, crashing down next to legs that jutted out at odd angles, while it tried to raise its heavy body higher and higher.

"Fuck!" she screamed.

Then she ran as fast as she could, keeping pace with the big man ahead of her. It was hard, running and balancing at the same time, but she did her best, periodically looking back to make sure that thing wasn't chasing them. If it wasn't dead yet, it sure as hell would be once this quake got through with it.

They ran forever, or at least what felt like it, until they approached thirty feet of stone jutting up in front of them at a 90-degree angle. The rope Titan secured in place with the grappling hook was still there, and without hesitation he grabbed it and started climbing.

"Come on," he yelled. "We don't have much time."

She waited until he was ten feet up, then took hold of the rope and started her own ascent. She grunted and cried out through gritted teeth as the sweat poured from every inch of her skin. Her muscles felt like Jell-O, but she wouldn't give up. Not after coming so close to the end. Not now.

An unexpected shift of rock caused her grip to falter, and she fell five feet before digging in with her boots. Even though she was wearing gloves, she could feel her palms burning, struggling to hang on to the rope. Above her, Titan had already made it to the top, yet he seemed so far away. Like the moon in the night sky.

But she used that as a beacon to draw herself closer and closer, as if his dim face was a port in a storm.

"Come on, you can do it!" he yelled, extending his hand. "You're almost there."

Emily felt the scream building deep within her. It started small, like a seed, and slowly sprouted through her lungs, weaving its way up her esophagus until it bore fruit in her throat, and she let it fly as she gave one last ditch effort to haul herself up and grab Titan's outstretched hand. Her fingers met his and for a fleeting moment she didn't think it would stick, and she saw herself tumbling down, down, down, head meeting stone, brains splattering all over the place like a cracked egg.

Then she was jolted upward, her arm nearly ripped from its socket.

She'd made it. Again.

Emily chanced a look down as Titan held onto her vest, and saw in the distance the spider still trailing after them, just as desperate as they were to escape the confines of the quaking earth.

Then he hauled her back, and together they started running.

CHAPTER 42

Hazelnut cranked the wheel to the right, narrowly avoiding a sinkhole that opened up. She looked in the rearview, and saw a Toyota Corolla that wasn't so lucky. The vehicle lurched, and fell into a hole. She had a chance to see the look of horror on the driver's face before he disappeared forever, swallowed whole by the planet.

The entire town was crumbling all around her. Houses cracked, businesses tumbled, and the roads opened wide to devour residents who weren't lucky enough to get to their cars fast enough—and even some who were, as evidenced by the unfortunate soul in the Corolla.

She could only attribute the earthquake to the massive explosion that rocked the mountain. For a blast of that caliber to come so soon after a natural quake, it was only logical to think it was cause and effect. An earthquake, a few aftershocks, and then things settle. Only this time the earth hadn't had a chance to rest, and with the combination of C4 and natural gas, well, you didn't have to be rocket scientist to figure out the damage those two things could do together, especially on unstable ground.

Christ, what a disaster. They'd done so much to save this place, and there it was behind her, folding in around itself like a house of cards.

She slammed her fists on the wheel. "Fuck!"

Beside her, Jim Albright looked over his shoulder at his wife, Karen, who was sitting white-knuckled in the backseat of their Outback. The pair had managed to make it to Mrs. Albright before things really started going to hell. They'd piled in the vehicle, and raced through town at breakneck speed. Hazelnut had made radio contact with Oral and Mr. Tempo to make sure they were safe, and they were.

But no one had heard from Emily and Titan.

Were they gone? Lost forever in the growing void beneath her? Hazelnut cringed, shaking her head at the thought before—

"Watch out!' Jim shouted.

She swerved, narrowly avoiding a Labrador that darted out in front of them.

"Fucking dogs," she grunted.

It's how this whole thing started: a dog. She'd be damned if that's how it would end for her.

"Almost there," she mumbled.

Ahead, the road leading out of Franklin was now free of the Bus. It was already clear, resting at the bottom of the mountain in the parking lot of Grant Memorial, awaiting her arrival.

She gave the Outback a little more gas just as two trees back and to her left toppled sideways, their roots exposed before they, too, were consumed by the earth. Hazelnut imagined there would be nothing left of Franklin once it was all over.

She was right.

CHAPTER 43

Emily followed Titan through the crack, which had remained wide open. She wasn't hopeful, but after catching sight of it in the distance her heart quickened and a last surge of adrenaline coursed through her, giving her the speed she needed to reach it. In the process, she even passed Titan, but her instincts as team leader took over and she allowed him to snake his way to safety before she made it through.

Shortly thereafter, the opening buckled, closing to two feet instead of four, and as they made their way out of the cave and atop the mountain, they got their first glance of what remained of Franklin.

"My God," she whispered.

"There's...there's nothing there," Titan blinked, rubbing his eyes for clarification.

Sure enough, he was right. There was now nothing where Franklin once stood. Just a large sinkhole filled with remnants of the town they'd tried so desperately to save. In the evening sky, just before the sun set completely, it wasn't hard to tell. Franklin was gone, and with it who knew how many residents that never had the chance to make it out alive. A hundred? Three hundred? And how many had fallen prey to the spiders before that?

Emily shook her head. She felt the corners of her eyes sting with tears, and she choked back a sob, crouching down with her elbows resting on her knees before she hit the ground completely, exhausted and angry.

"Hey," Titan said, his back to the cave. "We did the best we could. Don't blame yourself."

"Then who do I blame?" she asked, though not specifically to him, but to anyone that might be listening. God, the Universe, aliens?

Behind her, footsteps approached through the trees, and a voice said, "You blame those fucking bastards that killed my dog."

Emily quickly got to her feet, and watched as David Perry came into view. He wore camo pants, jacket, even a beanie, and his face was painted brown, black, and green to resemble the countryside. He carried a Remington bolt-action rifle in his hand, and a look of disdain on his face.

"Mr. Perry?" she asked, placing her palm on the barrel of Titan's SCAR, signifying that it was okay to lower his weapon.

"That's right. Followed you two up here a good long while ago, figured I'd hang out and see what you brought back. Looks like you got a whole lotta nothing. Ah well, least I wasn't down there. I imagine my trailer's pretty much done for."

"Yeah, I'd say that's a safe bet," Titan told him.

"Well, look at you," David said, approaching. "God damn you're a big one. Seal?"

"Delta. You serve?"

"Did two tours in Afghanistan after nine-eleven," Mr. Perry told him. "Army."

"Hooah," Titan grunted.

"Hoo-fuckin-ah." He looked at Titan's BDUs, the pockets, the baton, his rifle, all of it. "Ain't never wore anything like that, though."

Emily glanced once more at where Franklin used to be. She tapped her earbud, hoping it still worked, and said, "Cryptkeeper to anybody, do you copy? Is anyone still alive out there? Conductor? Oral?"

Through the static she heard Mr. Tempo's voice break through with a crackle before the interference cleared.

Cryptkeeper, this is Conductor. Welcome back.

She'd never been so happy to hear another person's voice in her life, and the tears that were threatening her eyes spilled out down her cheeks, though with them came a relieved laughter as she looked at Titan and nodded.

"Glad to be back, sir. Titan's with me."

That's good to hear. There's a rescue chopper en route to your last known position. I called Langley for help. All they know is that two government officials need assistance, so stay where you are and when they arrive, say nothing."

"Roger that, sir. Oral and Hazelnut, did they make it out?"

They did. They're with me now. We're at Grant Memorial where Charlotte has just administered a dose of antivenom to Tiffany Albright. Her parents are with her, and it looks like she's coming out of the woods.

"And her uncle?"

There was a brief pause, and Mr. Tempo said, *Sadly, he didn't make it.*

She didn't need to hear the details. Not yet. For now, she was glad the child was back with her mother, and the rest of the team was safe.

Did you find what you were looking for? Mr. Tempo asked.

"We did, and it's—"

Before Emily could say the word dead, a thunderous crash followed by a low hiss emerged from the cave, and the battered, bloody body of the spider crawled its way toward them. Her mouth dropped—a quiet, terrified squeak escaping her.

What happened next happened so fast, yet she saw it all in slow motion.

Titan whirled on the creature, raising the barrel of his rifle and pulling the trigger, but the weapon jammed. His expression changed to worried anger as he tried to fix it, but it was no use. As he reached for his sidearm, David Perry stepped up beside him, fired his Remington, cycled the bolt, and fired again.

It was no use.

Even with more of the spider's body exposed as the rock that'd grown like a shell around it cracked and chipped, falling away to reveal a gargantuan mass of flesh and blood, it still kept coming.

Emily felt like it would follow them to the ends of the earth if it had to.

But then Mr. Perry, in an act of either pure selflessness, or pure stupidity—she wasn't sure which—grabbed a frag grenade hanging off Titan's belt. He pulled the pin, and charged the spider with everything he had in him, screaming, "For Buckeye!"

The beast opened its jaws, and before David could toss the grenade down its throat, the creature clamped onto his arm, ripping the limb off at the shoulder. Blood spurted like a fountain as he screamed, turning to reveal a face that had drained of all color, leaving behind a ghostly white skin tone as he started to go into shock. The spider clapped down hard again, piercing his spine. Its fangs protruded through his chest, and more blood gushed out Mr. Perry's mouth, gurgling and spurting down his chin and to his chest.

Titan sprang toward Emily, screaming, "Get down," as he tackled her to the ground, landing hard on top her. She felt a sharp crack as the air rushed from her lungs, and she had a moment to look up at the stars before an explosion rocked the earth beneath her. The next thing she knew it was pouring down rock, and blood, and bits of human flesh mixed with prehistoric chunks of spider.

But it was over.

Mr. Perry sacrificed himself to save them, or to preserve the memory of his beloved animal, or to get revenge on the bastards that killed his dog. Whatever the reason, she was grateful.

When Titan rolled to the side, Emily sat up, her arm hanging limp and broken across her stomach. She glanced toward the east, and saw the spotlight of a helicopter off in the distance growing closer.

CHAPTER 44

Mr. Tempo stood at the head of a large conference table in a dimly lit room in a nondescript building near the Philadelphia Regional Port Authority. Across the table, seated at the other end, Michelle Liu rested her hands atop a file folder that sat next to a projector. To his left, Oral and Hazelnut were sitting beside Hackman, whose knee bounced nervously up and down as he sipped on a Mountain Dew.

To Mr. Tempo's right, and next to an empty chair, Titan waited patiently, his fingers laced together and in his lap as he glanced toward the door before checking his watch.

In the middle of the table, pitchers of water and cans of soda took up space next to a platter of turkey and ham sandwiches that no one had touched since taking their seats.

After a few more minutes of uncomfortable silence, Tempo cleared his throat and said, "I think we'll start with—"

The door to the conference room opened. Light seeped in from the hallway, casting long shadows across the floor. Emily Nite stepped over the threshold, her left arm in a thick cast that engulfed her thumb but let her fingers breathe. It hung in a sling draped across her shoulder, and as she limped into the room Titan stood and pulled out her chair.

She took a seat next to Mr. Tempo. "Sorry I'm late."

A brief smile touched his lips. "It's okay, we were just getting started."

Titan pushed her closer to the table, and she shifted, making herself as comfortable as she could.

It'd been a week since West Virginia, and they'd been called to an informal review of the events that took place in Franklin.

Emily had spent the better part of her time recuperating from various bruises and aches, as well as the broken arm received, unintentionally, at the hands of Titan. She'd kept in contact with her team, but this was the first time they'd all been in the same room together since that horrible day.

"Now then," Mr. Tempo began. "I think it best we start with Miss Liu. Michelle, would you be so kind as to go over with the team your findings from the initial tests done on the spider carcass we managed to preserve?"

"Certainly," she said, standing.

Dressed in a pair of jeans and a white sweatshirt, her black hair hung down just past her shoulders. Emily watched her start the digital projector, which beamed a 72-inch rectangular screen across the wall behind Oral, Hazelnut, and Hackman.

The first image displayed was that of the dead spider, sliced and spread open to reveal its inner workings.

Emily shuddered. Those things were all she could see when she closed her eyes at night, and she wondered if the others were experiencing the same post traumatic stress.

"After examining the creature, I discovered that it features lungs not unlike our own. This would indicate that modern day arachnids somehow evolved from these spiders, developing a breathing system more suited to current levels of oxygen in our atmosphere. This also lends weight to my theory that these were the first species in the order of Araneae to walk the earth."

"So they were dinosaurs?" Oral asked.

"Sort of." Michelle nodded. "That's the interesting part. After sequencing the genome, I found that only 26 percent of their DNA resembled anything even remotely close to the spiders we know today. The remaining 74 percent is unknown. I've never seen anything like it. It's so unlike any arachnid we've discovered that it could be called alien."

"Wait," Titan said. "So you're saying these things were alien dinosaurs?"

"Not alien in the sense that they came from another planet, just that we've yet to discover where they fit on the evolutionary ladder. They could be the first, but without anything to compare them to, it's hard to say."

"What else?" Mr. Tempo asked.

Michelle hit a button on the remote controlling the projector, and the image on the wall displayed a large chunk of debris from the giant spider Emily and Titan had discovered deep within the earth.

"The mother spider. Bigger than all the rest and infinitely more complex. Without a full-body carcass it was difficult to examine, but we had enough pieces to at least determine that Cryptkeeper's initial belief that the exoskeleton was made up of rock and mineral is correct. It'd been down there so long that the earth itself had formed to it, though when I managed to break through the tough exterior, it had the same flesh and blood as the others."

"Any guesses as to why the smaller creatures did not have this same exoskeleton?" Mr. Tempo asked.

"A few, the main one being that they were the workers, so they were always on the move. The mother sat in the same spot for long periods of time, giving it a chance to develop its hard shell made up of various materials found in the earth."

"Lazy bitch," Hazelnut quipped.

"Is that all, Miss Liu?"

"Yes, sir. For now, anyway. I'm going to continue extracting information, and I'll keep you updated as things progress."

"Fair enough." He turned to Hackman and said, "Mr. Collett, if you please."

John gulped back a long swallow of soda, and wiped his lips. He still looked the same as he did that day on the Bus. Smelled like it, too. His hair was a disheveled mess, and his clothes were wrinkled and rank. Emily could smell him from across the table.

"With the relocation of the remaining residents of Franklin, social media activity has been weak. There were a few that posted grainy images and shaky video from that day, but those were quickly intercepted and dealt with accordingly. As for those that have tried to go the media with the story, they've either been dismissed as unstable, or we've managed to lean on the right people enough for them to bury the lede, reporting it as nothing more than a fluff piece. The real story is the one we used to cover it up—a gas main explosion big enough to destabilize the earth after the initial quake two weeks ago that it opened a giant sinkhole and swallowed the town hole."

"That's messed up," Titan said, and everyone turned toward him. He met their gazes, his lips pressed firmly together as if he didn't realize he'd spoken out loud.

"Care to elaborate on that?" Mr. Tempo asked.

Titan shrugged. "Doesn't the world have a right to know what really happened?"

"That's rich coming from someone like you," Oral said.

"Someone like me?"

"Us, I mean. We've been on so many clandestine missions that I've lost count. If the world knew everything we've done in the name of freedom, don't you think they'd be a little horrified?"

"This is different," Titan grunted.

"No, it's not," Hazelnut chimed in. "Those things were a threat not just to Franklin, but the entire continent. We've taken out people that posed similar consequences. Just because these had eight legs doesn't make it any less significant. Do you really think it's in the best interest of everyone to know what really happened? Shit, before you know it there'd be religions popping up devoted to those fucking things, because people are just that stupid."

"I don't think—"

"Before things get out of hand," Mr. Tempo said, raising his hands to squelch the brewing argument, "I think it best we hear from Emily. After all, she's spent her entire life devoted to these types of discoveries, and now that you have definitive proof of the existence of giant spiders, Miss Nite, I'm curious: what do you plan to do with that information?"

Emily tapped a finger on the table, her lips pursed to the side as she chewed on the inside of her cheek. She met eyes with everyone around the table, finally landing on Titan.

"They're right," she said. "As much as I'd like to believe that the world would meet a discovery like this with open-minded wonder, I think a more reasonable response among the general population would be confusion, fear, and anger. People are afraid of what they don't understand. We've seen it in every Hollywood movie dealing with aliens, and to be honest I don't think that's far from the truth."

"So you're inclined to keep this close to the chest," Mr. Tempo said.

She nodded, still looking at Titan, and said, "We have our answers, as many as we can for the time being. That's enough for me, and it should be enough for you."

He stared back at her, his expression blank yet contemplative. After a few beats, he grinned and said, "You're the boss."

"About that," Mr. Tempo quickly added, and Emily turned her attention toward him. "We all know this was a trial run for Miss Nite, and in a lot of ways it was for all of us. What I'd like to know now is if this is something everyone would like to be a part of going forward. Now, I know mistakes were made, and though we lost a lot of good, innocent people, our mission was accomplished. We stopped those creatures from spreading, and after speaking to the president, he agrees. This was a success, despite evidence to the contrary."

"Hell yeah," Hackman said without hesitation. "This is the most fun I've had in, well, forever."

"Fun?" Oral asked. "You think that was fun?"

"Hey, when you spend your days cooped up in front of a computer like I do, any chance to do some good is fun."

"Kid," Oral said, "we need to get you laid." A chorus of chuckles erupted around the table, which the soldier promptly slapped before saying, "I'm in, for sure."

"Me too," Hazelnut agreed.

"Yeah," Titan nodded. "I'm good to go."

Michelle raised her hand and said, "I know I was brought in for just this mission, but if you need anymore help in the future, feel free to give me a call."

"Appreciated," Mr. Tempo said. He looked to Emily, as did everyone else around the table. Then he said, "Miss Nite?"

She couldn't stop thinking about all those people. So many of them dead and buried beneath the rubble of a town they once called home. Her team failed to save the majority of them, and while those above her might've considered the mission a success, she couldn't see it that way. Their screams would haunt her for the rest of her life, just like the screams of war haunted her father.

Look what became of him, she thought.

But she wasn't her father, and she vowed to herself she never would be.

There was redemption to be had, and there was only one way to get it.

Her lips parted, and she said, "I know I'm not the strongest leader, yet, but if you'll have me I'd like to stay on with the team."

Nods of approval met her words. Titan took hold of her shoulder and gave it a quick squeeze. "You'll get there, boss," he said.

"Yes, you will," Mr. Tempo agreed. "And as such, I'll have a less commanding presence for the next mission, allowing you all to get used to Miss Nite as your commanding officer. Any issues will be reported to her. Any concerns, questions, and feedback will be delivered to Emily, not to me. Are we clear?"

"Clear," Titan said.

"Definitely." Oral and Hazelnut nodded.

"You got it," Hackman said.

"Good." Mr. Tempo cracked a smile. "Then I'd officially like to welcome you all to the newly formed Department of Anomalies."

"DOA." Emily laughed. "That has a nice ring to it."

"Indeed," Mr. Tempo said.

"Wait," Oral raised his chin, "you said you'll have less of a commanding presence during the next mission. Is there another mission?"

Mr. Tempo reached down toward the floor and pulled his leather attaché up to the table. He opened it, eyeballed everyone with a mischievous gleam in his eyes, and pulled out a file folder.

"As a matter of fact," he said, "there is."

SEVEREDPRESS

facebook.com/severedpress
twitter.com/severedpress

CHECK OUT OTHER GREAT HORROR NOVELS

BLACK FRIDAY
by Michael Hodges

Jared the kleptomaniac, Chike the unemployed IT guy, Patricia the shopaholic, and Jeff the meth dealer are trapped inside a Chicago supermall on Black Friday. Bridgefield Mall empties during a fire alarm, and most of the shoppers drive off into a strange mist surrounding the mall parking lot. They never return. Chike and his group try calling friends and family, but their smart phones won't work, not even Twitter. As the mist creeps closer, the mall lights flicker and surge. Bulbs shatter and spray glass into the air. Unsettling noises are heard from within the mist, as the meth dealer becomes unhinged and hunts the group within the mall. Cornered by the mist, and hunted from within, Chike and the survivors must fight for their lives while solving the mystery of what happened to Bridgefield Mall. Sometimes, a good sale just isn't worth it.

GRIMWEAVE
by Tim Curran

In the deepest, darkest jungles of Indochina, an ancient evil is waiting in a forgotten, primeval valley. It is patient, monstrous, and bloodthirsty. Perfectly adapted to its hot, steaming environment, it strikes silent and stealthy, it chosen prey: human. Now Michael Spiers, a Marine sniper, the only survivor of a previous encounter with the beast, is going after it again. Against his better judgement, he is made part of a Marine Force Recon team that will hunt it down and destroy it.

The hunters are about to become the hunted.

SEVEREDPRESS

 facebook.com/severedpress
 twitter.com/severedpress

CHECK OUT OTHER GREAT HORROR NOVELS

DEATH CRAWLERS
by Gerry Griffiths

Worldwide, there are thought to be 8,000 species of centipede, of which, only 3,000 have been scientifically recorded. The venom of Scolopendra gigantea—the largest of the arthropod genus found in the Amazon rainforest—is so potent that it is fatal to small animals and toxic to humans. But when a cargo plane departs the Amazon region and crashes inside a national park in the United States, much larger and deadlier creatures escape the wreckage to roam wild, reproducing at an astounding rate. Entomologist, Frank Travis solicits small town sheriff Wanda Rafferty's help and together they investigate the crash site. But as a rash of gruesome deaths befalls the townsfolk of Prospect, Frank and Wanda will soon discover how vicious and cunning these new breed of predators can be. Meanwhile, Jake and Nora Carver, and another backpacking couple, are venturing up into the mountainous terrain of the park. If only they knew their fun-filled weekend is about to become a living nightmare.

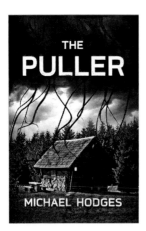

THE PULLER
by Michael Hodges

Matt Kearns has two choices: fight or hide. The creature in the orchard took the rest. Three days ago, he arrived at his favorite place in the world, a remote shack in Michigan's Upper Peninsula. The plan was to mourn his father's death and figure out his life. Now he's fighting for it. An invisible creature has him trapped. Every time Matt tries to flee, he's dragged backwards by an unseen force. Alone and with no hope of rescue, Matt must escape the Puller's reach. But how do you free yourself from something you cannot see?

 SEVEREDPRESS

 facebook.com/severedpress
 twitter.com/severedpress

CHECK OUT OTHER GREAT HORROR NOVELS

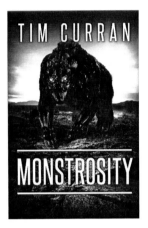

MONSTROSITY
by Tim Curran

The Food. It seeped from the ground, a living, gushing, teratogenic nightmare. It contaminated anything that ate it, causing nature to run wild with horrible mutations, creating massive monstrosities that roam the land destroying towns and cities, feeding on livestock and human beings and one another. Now Frank Bowman, an ordinary farmer with no military skills, must get his children to safety. And that will mean a trip through the contaminated zone of monsters, madmen, and The Food itself. Only a fool would attempt it. Or a man with a mission.

THE SQUIRMING
by Jack Hamlyn

You are their hosts.

You are their food.

The parasites came out of nowhere, squirming horrors that enslaved the human race. They turned the population into mindless pack animals, psychotic cannibalistic hordes whose only purpose was to feed them.

Now with the human race teetering at the edge of extinction, extermination teams are fighting back, killing off the parasites and their voracious hosts. Taking them out one by one in violent, bloody encounters.

The future of mankind is at stake.

And time is running out.

Made in United States
North Haven, CT
17 February 2023